The Winter Hare

The Winter Hare

Joan Elizabeth Goodman

MAP AND DECORATIONS BY THE AUTHOR

Houghton Mifflin Company
Boston 1996

For information about this and other Houghton Mifflin
trade and reference books and multimedia products,
visit The Bookstore at Houghton Mifflin on the
World Wide Web at http://www.hmco.com/trade/.

The text of this book is set in 12 point Janson Text.

Library of Congress Cataloging-in-Publication Data

Goodman, Joan E.
The winter hare / Joan Elizabeth Goodman.
p.   cm.
Summary: In 1140, with England divided between the supporters
of King Stephen and those of the Empress Matilda, twelve-year-old
Will Belet, small for his age but longing to be a knight,
comes to his uncle's castle to be a page and soon finds himself
involved in dangerous intrigues and adventures.
ISBN 0-395-78569-3
1. Great Britain — History — Stephen, 1135–1154 — Juvenile fiction.
[1. Great Britain — History — Stephen, 1135–1154 — Fiction.
2. Knights and knighthood — Fiction.   3. Middle Ages — Fiction.]
I. Title.
PZ7.G61375Wi   1996   95-53844
[Fic] — dc20   CIP   AC

Printed in the United States of America
BP   10   9   8   7   6   5   4   3   2   1

Acknowledgments

In writing this book, I've depended on the work of many scholars, historians, and writers of fiction who've helped me visualize a time and place that is truly long ago and far away.

I'd also like to acknowledge my ninth-grade English teacher, Mrs. Ella Demers, who encouraged my writing and introduced me to the Middle Ages through Bryher's *The Fourteenth of October*.

Although *The Winter Hare* is indebted to the past it is dedicated to the future.

To Juliet Eve and Henry Michael — may the years ahead bring them countless blessings.

Contents

Preface

The year is 1140. England is ravaged by civil war between the supporters of Empress Matilda, daughter of King Henry, and Stephen of Blois, reigning king of England.

The seeds of conflict were sown in 1120 when King Henry's only son, Prince William, died in the disastrous sinking of *The White Ship*. King Henry hoped for another son with his new bride, but it was not meant to be.

When the German emperor died, Henry summoned his widowed daughter, Matilda, home to England. He named her Lady of England, and all the barons of the land swore to support her and see her issue crowned king. When King Henry died in December of 1135 in Normandy, he left Matilda to rule until her son, Henry Plantagenet, should be of age. But the barons didn't honor their pledge to King Henry. Stephen of Blois, Henry's nephew, hastened across the Channel and was able to gather enough supporters in London that the archbishop crowned him king by Christmas Day. For five years since that black day, England has been torn apart by those who accepted Stephen and those who remained loyal to King Henry and his heir.

The Winter Hare

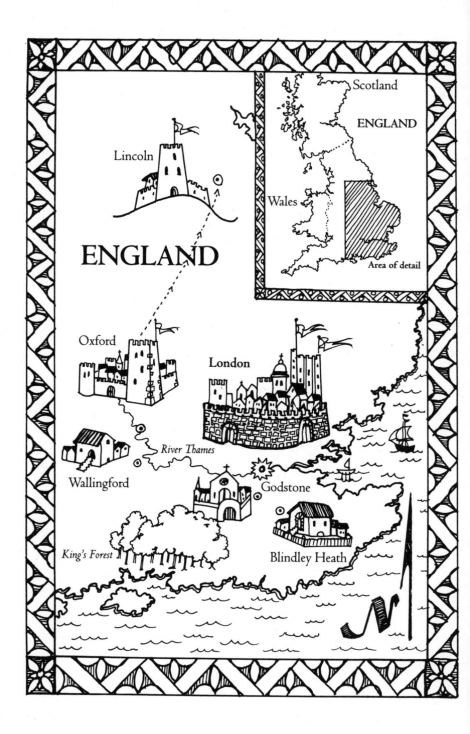

Lincoln

ENGLAND

Scotland

ENGLAND

Wales

Area of detail

Oxford

London

Wallingford

River Thames

Godstone

King's Forest

Blindley Heath

I.
Leave-taking

"Master Will! Tell your noble father the baggage is near readied." Peter of Redvers grinned at Will. "We await his leave to mount up. In haste, Will, are we not eager to set out?"

"Aye," said Will. "In haste!"

He ran across the bailey, deeply shadowed in pre-dawn gloom, yet more crowded than at the busiest midday. Horses stamped impatiently, and knights and villeins of the manor jostled each other as they made ready for the journey. The great hall was dark and empty of all but the crone who warmed her bones by the hearth and polished silver goblets until they mirrored her toothless grin. Will nodded as he ran past her. He ducked behind the carved oaken screen, and raced up the flimsy wooden stairs, lit by smoking torches, to the solar, his family's private chamber. There he'd find Sir John taking his leave of his mother and sisters. The wooden treads bounced underfoot.

1

Might he not bound up the stairs in a single leap, there was such excitement in him this day of leave-taking.

Torchlight flickered in the unnaturally silent room. His mother's women with their spindles and the little girls who had left off their play stared wide-eyed at Lady Alice and Sir John Belet. Will's parents were twined in each other's arms, their lips in a lasting kiss. When they finally parted, their eyes held each other, still. Will cleared his throat and broke the spell. Lady Alice flushed crimson and Sir John turned to Will.

"Peter of Redvers says the baggage is near readied."

"Then we shall be off," said Sir John. He formally kissed Joan and Margaret on their brows and lifted Agnes the Magpie high in the air, tickling her until she wriggled and squealed. Then he set her down and solemnly kissed her hand. He bowed to Lady Alice and she curtsied to the ground.

"Be not overlong," said Sir John, patting Will's shoulder as he went down to his men in the yard.

Will's mother came forward and wrapped him in her arms. Normally he would have shied away, but now Will stood quietly, engulfed in her gentle embrace and the scent of cloves.

"Will, my son, go forth in joy and strength. May Our Merciful Lady bring you through the evils that beset England to the safety of Oxford Castle, as she brought you safely through the pox."

2

It might be blasphemy, but Will trusted his father would lead them safely to Oxford with or without the Blessed Virgin Mary's help. Just as it had been his mother's skill with healing herbs and her patience as a nurse that had given him back his health.

"Study hard, Little Rabbit, and my stepbrother, Aubrey de Vere, will make a knight of you. You know there hasn't always been accord between your father and your uncle the earl . . ."

His mother need not remind him. Will knew quite well that the earl had a great enmity for Will's father, begun long ago by the earl's jealousy of the old-landed families whose claim to the weal of England was so much greater than his own. Blindley Heath had belonged to Will's family since the long-ago Saxon times. Will was proud of his heritage, and proud that Blindly Heath owed allegiance to no lord but the king.

Aubrey de Vere's father was a penniless knight without land or family who'd been given the hand of the wealthy widow, Countess de Vere, as reward for his service to the king. Aubrey succeeded to the title of earl only because Lady Alice had no brothers. Earl Aubrey never forgot his high estate, nor could he forget his humble origins. It seemed to gall him particularly that his brother-in-law, John Belet, held such a modest estate and yet was Earl Aubrey's equal in the realm.

Lady Alice kept Will at arm's length and spoke with

much seriousness. "I trust your good endeavors as those of your brother, John, will further mend the rift twixt my stepbrother and my lord."

Will nodded.

"Forget not what you have learned at *my* side. A noble knight needs to know both the arts of war and peace."

A noble knight. All Will had ever wanted for as far back as he could remember was to be a knight as noble and valorous as those in the jongleurs' tales. Could a "little rabbit" ever become such a knight as Roland? As Charlemagne? As the knights of King Arthur?

"Will, promise you will keep up with your Latin studies. Lady Elaine will be pleased if her new cup-bearer can also serve as a scribe."

"I promise," said Will. "Every day, I will read from the book you've given me."

"Write to me of your progress," said his mother.

"As often as I can," said Will.

His mother released him and stepped back a pace.

"I am trying to memorize you," she said. "For I fear, in these evil times . . . there is such a great danger . . . oh, my son, it will be long before I see you again."

Tears spilled out of her sea-green eyes and coursed down her pale cheeks onto her wimple.

"Faith!" she said, drying her eyes. "It is good your father is in the bailey and cannot see me weeping like a silly wench. Come, now, kiss your little sisters good-bye."

The girls abandoned their toys and crowded round him. Joan and Margaret hung on his arms and Agnes fastened herself round his leg. He tickled the older ones and hoisted Agnes up onto his hip.

"Look well on them," said his mother. "They will be busy growing while you are in Oxfordshire. Remember them as the sweet doves they are now."

At that, Agnes started to howl.

"I want to go too," she sobbed, pummeling Will with her fat little fists.

Will laughed and hugged her tight.

"Sweet little dove!"

"Hush now," said Lady Alice. She took Agnes in her arms and soothed her.

Will remembered bawling just as loudly to go with John when he'd left for Oxfordshire. That was when John was nine and Will was four. But even at four he'd been furious to be held behind while John went off on his great adventure. His oldest sister, Alice, had gone to the castle of her betrothed in Bristol when she was ten. And Edna, the second sister, went to the nuns at Woldingham when she was only eight. Always Will was left behind. When at last Will turned nine and it was his turn to go out in the world, to start on the path to knighthood, he'd been stricken with the pox. He'd had to wait three long years to be well enough, strong enough to serve as a page to his uncle Earl Aubrey de Vere. First page, then squire, then, God willing, he'd earn his spurs and be knighted. And then he could go out into the world and win fame and glory! His dream of leave-taking was finally coming true. As glad as he was to go, it was hard to say good-bye.

Agnes was whimpering softly as Will took his final leave. He *would* remember them like this; his mother holding Agnes, Joan, and Margaret at either side, all of them looking out from their fair, freckled faces, their green eyes darkened and grave.

The bailey was, if anything, more tumultuous than before, as the men made last-minute preparations. Pages and servants and villeins ran in and out of the storerooms with pieces of equipment. Cloaks were flung over leather hauberks whose bright metal disks sparkled in the dawn light. Armorers and squires bore gleaming swords, pikes, and shields blazing with bands of scarlet on quartered fields of blue and gules, the device of Sir John Belet. Horses whinnied and shook their reins. Hounds leapt around their handlers, yelping and snapping. All were restive and ready to be off.

The smith and the stable hands checked the packhorses, making sure all was in order. Two horses were required just to carry the presents for the earl and countess of Oxford. Will's mother was sending many fine linens, a set of bed curtains, and embroidered hangings for Lady Elaine. Vessels of silver and bronze, furs and rugs, plus all the trappings Will would need for his training, were strapped onto the horses.

Sir John stood by the mews, stroking the feathers of

his favorite falcon and speaking quietly with his steward and the knights who would stay behind to guard the manor. Even with all the shouts and confusion, it was his deep, calm voice that Will heard in the bailey.

Now the women came out from the kitchens, their veils fluttering wildly in the morning's breeze. Mildred, the beekeeper's daughter, shyly approached Will with a carefully sewn oilcloth package.

" 'Tis a honeycomb," she whispered, "to sweeten your path."

Mildred ducked her head and scurried away before Will could even say thank you.

Fat Gwen, the cook, caught Will up in a stranglehold.

"My little rabbit, leaving without a kiss for old Gwen?"

Will squirmed and struggled, trying to break away from her fat, grease-stained arms.

"Why so shy, *Little* Rabbit?" said Ranulf d'Artois, a young knight in his father's service who seemed to take great pleasure in bedeviling Will, especially about his small size. "Give the wench her due!"

"Aye, 'tis true, good sir," said Gwen, nodding her head and setting her chins to wobbling. "I'm only wanting my pay. You'd think this carrot-top rapscallion would be a might bigger for all the sweetmeats he's stolen from my larder."

While Gwen was talking to d'Artois, Will managed

to jab her with his elbow and escape, only to be caught up short by the steely grasp of d'Artois.

"Give the fair maid her kiss, Rabbit."

Will wriggled and kicked. How was it possible on this day of days to be so shamed in his father's presence?

"Mount up, Master Will," said Peter of Redvers, looking coldly at d'Artois. "Don't keep your good father waiting."

D'Artois dropped Will and strode off to his own horse. D'Artois seemed to live under a glowering sky. Although the manor was a crowded place, d'Artois kept to himself, remaining aloof from the close warmth and cheer in the hall. But, in spite of his dark moods, Will knew that his father valued d'Artois's knightly skills and steadfast honor. Will scrambled to his feet and onto his dappled mare. He guided her into his place in line between Peter of Redvers and Ranulf d'Artois.

They rode in single file through the gatehouse, the horses' hooves thundering over the narrow wooden bridge. Once on the road they reformed their ranks, riding three abreast and gathering speed. They passed the cottages and crofts where villeins grew leeks, beans, and cabbages. Women stood at their doors, holding babes, and waved. The villeins and their oxen, the cottagers carrying mattocks and hoes lined the road. John Belet was well loved by his tenants. Even during this savage time, when many starved, no one lacked for food or shelter in Sir John Belet's demesne. The peasants waved their ox-goads and shouted "Hurrah!" as their lord and his men passed by. Will drew a deep breath of the new autumn morning. The still-green meadows sparkled in the first light of day. Haystacks dotted the fields and the earth, newly ploughed for the winter crops, yielded up its dark, rich scent. The road ahead was long. Will sat high on his pretty mare and forgot for the moment the humiliations of Ranulf d'Artois and fat Gwen.

Then he glanced back over his shoulder. At the open casement of the solar was the pure white veil of his mother. Will knew her eyes were fixed on him.

"Good-bye," he whispered, then turned back in his saddle to face the road stretching out before him. He would work hard. He'd make up for the lost years and bring great honor to his family. He sat up straighter in the saddle. He would make Lady Alice proud.

Only a small band was traveling from Blindley Heath in Surrey; Sir John wanted to leave his manor and lands there as well defended as possible. Geoffrey de Mandeville, earl of Essex, or some other greedy baron, would hasten to lay siege to an ill-defended demesne. The lawlessness of King Stephen's reign encouraged such black deeds. Sir John and his men would travel north to a fief that Sir John held in the king's forest near Woldingham. There, five armed knights and their squires who owed fealty to Sir John would join them for the journey to Oxfordshire.

His father mocked his own precautions, saying that in the late King Henry's day, a lady carrying a babe could walk the length and breadth of England unharmed. But since Stephen usurped the throne from Empress Matilda, rightful Lady of England, even an old, hardened warhorse like himself must watch his shadow as he stepped foot outside his manor.

Will knew that the extra knights were deemed necessary in part because of him — it was feared his little mare wouldn't be able to outrun a band of robbers. And Lady Alice had insisted that they have extra men as it was well known the earl of Essex preyed upon travelers in Surrey and Kent, filling his coffers with their gold and his dungeons with new victims.

Sir John said that Lady Alice wanted the extra knights to make a fine showing for Will's arrival at her stepbrother's great castle. But his father said that to tease his mother and make light of the danger.

They rode fast and were soon beyond his father's fields and woods, the parish church and villages Will knew so well. And once they turned onto the old Roman road that ran from Lewes to London, Will's adventure had truly begun. A stretch of the king's forest lay ahead. Sir John planned to take a doe or boar — if he could. They would bring their kill to

Godstone and have their dinner in the abbey there.

Will had never been on a real hunt, and never in the king's forest. At most, he'd scared up a badger and some hares in his father's woods with some of the boys from the village. The king's forest was much grander than the woods at Blindley Heath, covering nearly half of Surrey, although in the Saxon days, a goodly portion of the forest had belonged to Blindley Heath. The king's forests were mostly comprised of lands William the Conqueror had taken from Saxon lords. Sir John said the forest stretched over one-third of the country and would be the ruination of England. Once the peasants had been able to hunt in the forest and supplement their table during the harshest times. Now they would be hanged for snaring a hare or lose an arm for taking greenwood. Only the king and his barons could hunt in the forests, and the barons had to pay for the pleasure.

But Will thought it was wonderful. All the wildest beasts lived in the king's forests — bears, wild cats, boars, and wolves. And in the largest forests in the deepest glades lived the unicorn! Will shivered with the thrill of it.

"Frightened, Little Rabbit?" said d'Artois.

"Let the boy be," said Peter of Redvers.

D'Artois snickered. "But a rabbit is such easy prey," he said.

"Pay him no heed," said Peter to Will. "D'Artois

was born with thorns which he must inflict on others."

Will smiled. Even the black-browed d'Artois wouldn't ruin this day.

The air was pierced with the silver cry of Sir John's hunting horn. The verderers and foresters were fairly warned that a lord of the land had come to hunt.

The horses were slowed to an easy gait as they entered the greenwood single file. Will's first hunt had begun.

II.
The Hunt

The vert gave way to deeper, older forest where great oaks stretched heavenward, dressed in autumn's colors. Sir John signaled for them to stop. Two knights were chosen to keep watch over the packhorses. Sir John turned his steady gaze to Will, who held his breath in terror lest he, too, would have to miss out on the chase.

"Have you no weapon, boy?" asked Sir John.

"I've a bow, sir. It's on the packhorse."

"As if he'd have the skill to use it," said d'Artois under his breath.

"Ranulf d'Artois," said Sir John quietly.

"My liege," said d'Artois.

"I would have you stay behind with the horses. It wouldn't do for milady's treasures to be carted off by a chance poacher."

"But, my lord —"

"D'Artois! I need a man of *your* skill to stay behind."

"As you will, my lord," said d'Artois, his dark face reddening.

"Well, young Will. Fetch your bow," said Sir John. "The hounds are eager to be off."

The dogs *were* excited. They pranced around their keeper, tangling their leads and yelping. The huntsman, his boy, and the dog handlers led them away into the deeper vert to find a scent and flush out the game. Will dismounted, retrieving his bow and a quiver of arrows from one of the packhorses. He strung his bow and slung the quiver on his back, sneaking only the briefest glance at the glowering d'Artois. There but for the grace of our Lord, stay I, thought Will as he mounted his mare. Peter of Redvers grinned at him, and Will was suddenly so excited and anxious, he nearly yelped like the dogs.

In a short while the huntsman's boy returned to the clearing. The huntsman had found tracks of a doe, and the hounds had caught the scent. With a nod from Sir John, Peter of Redvers sounded the oliphant, signaling the keeper to let loose his hounds. The horn rang through the forest. Will felt his mare tense. He held his reins tightly. For one brief moment, all the men and horses held perfectly still, poised on the brink of the hunt.

The oliphant sounded again. Will spurred his mare, and the party raced forward as one. The chase was on!

Will was in the lead and soon spotted the hounds,

running through the deep vert and howling like mad. The hooves of the warhorses pounded the forest floor behind him. But he dared not look around. Will kept his head down and his eyes on the ground. He hugged his mare, whispering in her ear, "You'll have your fill of oats and apples if only you'll match the pace and keep your footing."

They raced through heavy forest. Branches caught at Will's cloak and breeches, threatening to pull him off. But he clung to the mare, and she held steady to the wild course set by the hounds. Directly in front of Will was a brindled bitch. Will concentrated on her, and it helped him keep his head and his seat. The men shouted at each other and their horses.

"Steady on!"

"Out of my way!"

"Watch out!"

"Watch out, yourself!"

The mare sailed over fallen branches and scarcely missed a step on the rough ground. Will heard a loud crash, a horse's neigh, and men's laughter. Someone was down. They soon came to a clearing, and now the hounds' voices rose to a frenzied pitch. Across the broad field, on the edge of a thicket, Will could just make out the shape of a doe.

"Now," cooed Will in the mare's ear. "As fast as you can, as fast —"

"*Halt!*" shouted Sir John.

Will pulled his mare up short and nearly toppled off. Now he could hear the horn. A shrill cry of alarm came from the forest they'd left. The men with packhorses were in danger. Will swung his mare around and joined the others, racing back through the forest to their aid.

As they neared the greenwood, Will heard the clash of steel and the frightened whinny of horses. The knights put on their helmets and drew their swords as they rode. Peter of Redvers slowed his horse long enough to pull alongside Will.

"Stay back from the fighting, Master Will," he said. "Will!"

"Yes, sir."

At least ten knights were swarming around Sir John's men and the packhorses. Will recognized the black and crimson of their shields as those of the earl of Essex. D'Artois, with his back to the packhorses, was fighting off two of the knights. As they drew closer one of Essex's men raised high his sword, bringing it down on the shoulder of Gilbert of Godalming. Gilbert fell from his horse, blood pouring out of him and soaking the ground.

Sir John filled the air with a terrible cry. Charging into the midst of the battle, he struck a mortal blow to the murderous knight. He wheeled around, and his avenging sword sought out the enemy.

Meanwhile, his men had closed in on Essex's knights. The clamor of sword on sword on shield was deafening. Occasionally there were animal-like shouts of anger or pain, but no words. Will stayed back as he'd been told. He'd often heard the minstrels tell of great battles and bloodshed. Now, in the thick of it, he longed to be any place else *except* this bloody glade.

Gilbert of Godalming lay on his back, exposed to the battle raging above him. Will wished he could protect him from the trampling horses or, at least, stop the ceaseless flow of his blood.

Blood splattered on shields and dripped from sword arms. Peter of Redvers had been struggling with a knight nearly twice his size. He made a deft turn on his horse, threw the knight off balance, and struck his head from his body. The head rolled on the ground to within a few feet of Will. It looked up at him with wide, angry, unseeing eyes.

The world seemed to go all black and red. Will leaned as far forward as possible, twining his fingers in his mare's mane, shutting his eyes, shutting out this horror.

When he looked again, Sir John and his knights were headed out of the forest toward the road, pursuing the knaves of Essex. The fighting was over. The wood was still but for the lone cry of a woodcock. Four knights were on the ground. The packhorses and chargers stood like statues. The wood was so quiet. It couldn't be real. It must be a dream, a terrible vision . . .

"Help me!"

It was real.

Will slid off his mare and ran to help.

D'Artois was hurt. Blood flowed from his shield arm and left thigh.

"Bind the wounds," he said.

Will nodded. Yes, the blood must be stopped. But with what? He ran to the packhorse and pulled out one of the treasures for the earl of Oxford. It was wrapped in white linen. The linen would do. Will dumped a silver basin on the ground and ran back to d'Artois.

"The leg is worse than the arm," said d'Artois. "Cut away the hose." And he handed Will his dagger.

Will cut away the bloodied leather, trying to be as gentle and quick as possible. He'd seen his mother tend injuries of the villeins, and he knew what must be done. If only he could do it. His hands were so clumsy. And the blood kept pouring out of the wound. What if the dagger slipped and he did d'Artois a greater injury? Will said a silent prayer to St. Damian, the physician.

The leather hose was cut free. Will cut the linen in strips and began to wind it around the wound.

"Tighter," said d'Artois, his teeth clenched and his face ashen with pain.

At last the bleeding was stanched. Will tied off the bandage as neatly as he could and looked to the wounded arm.

"Best take off the mail," said d'Artois.

Will helped him to a sitting position. He unlaced the leather jerkin and eased d'Artois out of the cumbersome mail. Sweat poured off d'Artois's brow as Will picked pieces of metal out of the wound. He tried to be as quick as possible. D'Artois was looking deathly. Finally the wound was clear, and he bound it up with the linen strips.

D'Artois sighed deeply and leaned back against an oak. Will's hands were sticky with d'Artois's blood. His tunic and cloak were streaked with red. His head began to spin. God grant he would not swoon like a woman.

"Master Will!" D'Artois brought him back to his senses. "Go to the packhorses and fetch us some wine."

As long as he had something to do Will felt he'd be all right. It was when he thought about the blood . . . better not to think. He found a flagon of wine and brought it to d'Artois, who drank deeply.

"You drink too, boy," he said. "It will steady you."

Will took a long drink and handed the flagon back to d'Artois.

"Is Gilbert alive?" asked d'Artois.

Will looked to the fallen knight. Gilbert lay in a pool of his own blood so thick it looked black. His mouth was open and his eyes gazed heavenward. A fly rested on his cheek.

19

"Does he breathe?" asked d'Artois.

Will leaned closer. There was no breath, only the smell of death. Will turned away from the corpse and vomited wine the color of blood.

Hoofbeats shook the ground. Will wiped his mouth and eyes. Peter of Redvers was approaching.

"Master Will, to your horse," he shouted. "D'Artois, can you manage it?"

Will hurried to help d'Artois to his feet. In a minute, Peter of Redvers was there, breathing heavily.

"We have to hurry. There were more of Essex's men on the road. Sir John sent me to save you and the packhorses. We must get to Godstone."

Between them, they got d'Artois on his horse. Will leapt onto his mare. Peter caught up the reins of the packhorses and remounted.

"Not a word," said Peter. "And keep close!"

He led them into the woods along the same trail they'd begun the hunt. The hunt! What had happened to the huntsman and the hounds?

A horn sounded from the greenwood behind them.

"They're coming!" said Peter.

The hunt was on! The hunters were now the prey.

III.
The Weald

The shrill of horns pursued them. With each blast, Will felt panic rising like a black tide. How could they outdistance Essex's men with three packhorses in tow? Was Sir John faring better on the Roman Road? Had he defeated the knaves of Essex?

Peter of Redvers led them through the winding trails to the same clearing where they'd spotted the doe. But instead of racing across the open field, he took them deeper into the forest where the path grew so wild they were slowed to a walk. The slower they went, the more Will panicked. If the earl's men caught them they would be hacked to pieces, or worse, taken to Essex's dungeon. But Peter was leading, and all Will could do was follow and pray he wouldn't wind up as the earl's prisoner.

If Will were grown, they might stand and fight the knaves instead of running like rabbits. Then he remembered the battle. Now he was only fit to run. But someday he'd be a knight like Roland and *never* run.

At least Peter seemed to know the king's forest quite well. He wove them through the trees as deftly as a creature of the wood. At one point he brought them into a thicket that was so dense, Will was certain they'd never get out. But sure enough, there was a narrow alleyway that branched off and took them down a hill and onto a wider trail. They picked up speed, and suddenly Will noticed that the sound of the horns had become a faint murmur in the distance.

"We've lost them!" said Will.

Peter turned in his saddle, frowning, shushing Will . . . and then he winked.

They had lost them! For now. Will looked over his shoulder to see if d'Artois understood that they were, for the moment, out of danger. D'Artois was slumped forward, barely holding on.

Will spurred his mare until he was abreast of Peter.

"D'Artois," he mouthed to Peter.

Peter handed Will the packhorses' reins and rode back to d'Artois. He roused d'Artois, who managed to sit up in the saddle, looking pale as a wraith.

Peter came back to Will, took the packhorses' reins and led the horses off the main trail onto a narrow twisting path. Will listened for the cry of horns. Sometimes he felt sure they grew louder. If Essex's men could track them to this thicket, they'd be without hope.

The path became too dense for riders. Peter dismounted and signed for Will to do the same. D'Artois was so slumped over on his horse that the low-hanging branches brushed lightly over him. And then they came to a tiny clearing.

In the center of the clearing was a ring of stones and the charred remains of a fire.

"What is this place?" whispered Will.

"A poacher's den," said Peter as he tied up the horses. "Come, help me with d'Artois."

They slid him off his horse and set him gently on the ground by the stones. He came to as they settled him, his eyes wide and frightened.

"Rest easy," said Peter. "For the time being we are safe."

D'Artois closed his eyes and sighed.

"There's a cave behind those brambles," said Peter, pointing to a tangle of underbrush. "First we'll tend to d'Artois and then we'll explore it. Now fetch us some wine."

Will went to the packhorse, remembering the flagon he'd left in the greenwood near the corpse of Gilbert of Godalming. What would become of Gilbert's immortal soul, with neither prayers nor proper burial? Would the demons claim him as their own? Will found another flagon and brought it to Peter.

"Did you do this?" asked Peter, pointing to the bandage on d'Artois's leg.

"Aye," said Will. Had he made the injuries worse with his clumsiness?

"Did you clear the wounds before you bound them?"

Will nodded.

"Where did you learn to doctor?"

"I watched my mother," said Will. Had he killed d'Artois?

"Did you also watch Lady Alice brew her medicines?"

"Yes," said Will.

"It will stand you in good stead," said Peter of Redvers. "I think you've saved d'Artois's leg. 'Tis well done, Master Will. Your father will be proud that your first battle did not rob you of your wits."

He'd done well! But then, Peter hadn't seen him puking like a babe.

"Is my father all right?" asked Will.

"You need not worry about Sir John," said Peter. "It would take a hundred knaves to bring him down."

"How many of Essex's men were there?"

"There were a score, perhaps more. Your father can handle them. But then he must hasten back to Blindley Heath, for Essex will come after him, seeking revenge."

"He would lay siege to our manor?"

"Only if he finds it ill-defended," said Peter. "After I leave you at Godstone, I'll go on to Woldingham and summon the vassals of Sir John to come to his aid."

"Couldn't I come with you?"

"Nay, lad. There's too much risk, and I must ride hard and fast. Your job will be to guard the treasure and help the monks look after d'Artois."

So he'd be left with the baggage at Godstone. If he were grown, if he were a knight, he'd ride with Peter.

"Tomorrow I'll bring you to the monks, and then make haste to Woldingham."

Meanwhile, what was happening to his mother and sisters at Blindley Heath?

"Tomorrow?" said Will.

"Aye, tonight we'll stay here."

"In the forest?!" asked Will. But everyone knew the night forest was filled with demons and wolves!

"We shall be snug enough," said Peter. "You unload and tend to the horses and I will make sure our den is free of bears."

Bears!

The cave was small and very dirty. It certainly smelled as if a bear had holed up there. But now it belonged to Will Belet, Peter of Redvers, and Ranulf d'Artois.

First Will gathered some twigs and brushed out the animal droppings. Then he unloaded the packhorses, piling up the treasures and food stores in the cave. Finally, he unsaddled, groomed, and watered the horses at the stream that trickled by the cave. Meanwhile, Peter had taken his bow and gone off in search of their dinner. D'Artois slept soundly on the ground. Will kept watch over him, listening intently for the horns of pursuit or the stirrings of wild animals. Every twig that snapped sent him spinning around, heart racing. *This is not how knights behave*, thought Will, starting at every rustle of the weald. Roland the Valorous would stand guard without fear.

D'Artois groaned in his sleep. His wound was bleeding through the linen bandages. It must be changed soon, but Will dared not attempt it alone.

At last Peter returned. He brought a brace of rabbits and a pouch filled with herbs.

He dropped the rabbits and spread a linen kerchief on the ground near Will. One by one he laid out the different plants.

"Do you recognize them, Master Will?"

"Henbane, loosestrife, yarrow, and toadflax," said Will. These were plants his mother, Lady Alice, had often sent him to gather in the woods near the village and by the river.

"And how shall we prepare them?" asked Peter.

"In haste," said Will. "His leg is bleeding anew."

"So much for *my* lessons," said Peter.

Quickly they made up a potion of loosestrife and a poultice of yarrow and toadflax. D'Artois awoke, looking dazed and flushed.

"You'll feel better before long," said Peter.

D'Artois groaned and closed his eyes.

Will set to unwinding the old bandage.

"You've lost a great deal of blood," said Peter. "But this will help close the wound."

D'Artois groaned.

When the wound was revealed, Peter crushed a sprig of loosestrife so that its juice dripped into the wound. Then he applied the poultice and wrapped the leg with a fresh bandage.

Will watched carefully. All was just as his mother would have done. Peter gave d'Artois the potion of loosestrife mixed in a cup of wine. D'Artois drank it down. He said nothing and kept his eyes shut tight. The pain must have been very great.

"Prepare the henbane, Master Will."

Will crushed the leaves and stems of henbane onto a strip of linen, which he draped across d'Artois's forehead. Then they changed the dressing on his shield arm.

" 'Tis finely done, Master Will," said Peter, sitting back on his heels. "These skills will serve you well. Second sons must know many things to get by. D'Artois would do well to take a lesson from you. He wastes too much of himself in anger at being born too late. Mayhap he envies you your skills and your ready smile."

Actually, Will was a third son. An older brother had

died when Will was still a babe. John would inherit Blindley Heath and the smaller holdings of Sir John Belet at Woldingham and Grinstead. The girls would have dowries, and Will would get nothing but a bit of gold, perhaps enough to buy a horse. Compared to John, he would be poor, indeed. It had never worried Will, for that was the law of the land. If estates were divided up amongst the younger sons, soon there would be nothing left to divide. Besides, even an impoverished knight might still win glory.

Will looked up. The woods around them had melted to dark shadows etched with black. The sky, visible through the branches, was deepening violet.

"Night draws on," said Peter. "I think we'll risk a fire. Essex's men have long departed and it will warn off the wild beasts and keep the horses safe. Besides, I like my dinner cooked — don't you?"

Will nodded. A night in the forest *without* a fire was beyond imagining. As it grew darker and darker around them, Will edged closer to the flickering firelight. Beyond the fire, the weald rose up like the shades of dragons. He hoped Peter was right, that Essex's men had indeed gone. Even without them, there was much to fear in the forest.

They roasted the rabbits and ate them with flat bread from their stores. Peter hand-fed d'Artois in spite of his protests. Will's portion was too soon gone. It had been a *very* long time since breakfast.

D'Artois began to have some color to him. The herbs were working, and the meat was restoring his strength. He sat up and asked Peter what had happened. Peter explained how Sir John and his knights had chased the knaves of Essex out of the forest, only to run into a much larger contingent of them on the Roman road.

Maybe Will's father had made it back to Blindley Heath by now. If he hadn't, what would happen to his mother?

"I didn't see much of the fighting," said Peter. "Sir John was anxious about you two and his treasure."

"Better to worry about his demesne," said d'Artois.

"On the morrow," said Peter, "I will rouse Sir John's knights at Woldingham and the lords of Grinstead and Copley. Blindley Heath will be well defended and no cause for concern."

Peter sounded so sure. Will prayed *he* was right, and not the scowling d'Artois.

"No one wants Essex to get a foothold in Surrey," said Peter.

"Why doesn't King Stephen stop Essex?" asked Will.

"The king can't," said Peter.

"But a king is mightier than an earl," said Will.

"Not this king," said d'Artois. "Besides, now Essex is a supporter of King Stephen."

"Stephen is weak and indecisive," said Peter.

"Lords like Essex have taken advantage of his spine-lessness to ravage the country and fill their own coffers."

"Is that why Father supports Empress Matilda?" asked Will.

"The empress has the rightful claim to the throne. And her son, Lord Henry, is our hope for the future. Only he can bring lasting peace to England."

"Meanwhile, that highhanded she-devil will be sharing her throne with the Angevin dog!" said d'Artois.

"Angevin dog?" asked Will.

"Geoffrey of Anjou," said Peter.

"Surely you know Angevins and Normans have always been enemies," said d'Artois. "King Henry must have made a pact with Satan when he married his daughter to the count of Anjou!"

"But before King Henry's death all the barons, even Stephen of Blois, swore allegiance *twice* to Matilda, naming her Lady of England," said Peter.

"Allegiance to *her!* And to her *son!*" said d'Artois. "Not to the Angevin!"

"Well, Sir John Belet honors his oath!" said Peter of Redvers.

D'Artois grunted. "England is left with poor choices. If only Her Imperial Highness were worthier of her position. But it would be best of all if her son were grown."

D'Artois fell silent. The only sound was the crackling fire.

Will had heard his father arguing like this with his men and other lords, though he'd never paid much attention. Now he was out in the world of men, and it was time he did pay attention. He stared into the fire, trying to sort it out. Empress Matilda was the daughter of good King Henry. First she had been married to the German emperor, who died. Then King Henry had married her to Geoffrey of Anjou. The barons of England hated d'Anjou, and because of the marriage their support of the empress wavered. When she and Anjou separated, the barons renewed their vow to support her. But once she was reconciled with her husband and King Henry was in his grave, many of the English lords turned against her. There were shapes in the fire . . . almost like pictures. Will was growing drowsy watching the flames. Tomorrow he'd think about the Empress. . . .

"Come, Master Will," said Peter. "Help me get d'Artois to the cave."

Will struggled up and helped support d'Artois. They spread a rug on the ground and used some of the softer bundles for pillows. Peter would keep watch. As Will was settling himself on the ground, he felt a lump in his shirt. He pulled out the wrapped honeycomb Mildred had given him so long ago that morning. He remembered her shy smile and prayed she would be safe. He would keep the honeycomb, not to eat, but to remind him of all the sweetness of home. Will pulled his cloak over him and sighed. Spending the night in the forest wasn't so bad, after all.

Will sprang awake in a terror. The horses whinnied and pawed the ground. A distant cry echoed through the forest. Was it the huntsman of Essex? Would they be trapped in this cave?

There it was again. Not a huntsman's horn, but the lone, mournful howl of a wolf. Another wolf howled in reply. And another, and another. The horrible chorus swelled as more and more wolves joined in, growing louder as the wolfpack drew near!

IV.
Godstone

It was pitch dark when Peter of Redvers woke him.

The howling wolves had kept Will awake much of the night and invaded his dreams as he slept. The last thing he wanted to do was ride out into their midst.

"But what about the wolves?" said Will.

"I am more worried about the earl of Essex than the wolves," said Peter. "We must get to Godstone by daybreak."

Reluctantly, Will helped make ready for their departure. The horses needed to be fed, watered, and saddled. The packhorses had to be loaded up again with all the supplies and presents for the earl of Oxford. Peter and Will helped d'Artois out of the cave and onto his charger.

"Did you enjoy the wolves' lullaby, Little Rabbit?" asked d'Artois with a mean smile.

"This little rabbit saved your leg," said Peter, "and perhaps your life. It ill becomes you to tease him."

33

D'Artois snorted.

Will had had so much to worry about it wasn't until he was mounted on his mare and they were riding away from the campsite that he thought of something even worse than wolves and Essex.

"The demons are abroad!" said Will. "We can't go through the weald while the devil reigns!"

D'Artois laughed out loud.

"Lad, those are stories nurses and clerics use to frighten the little children," said Peter. "If we fall into the hands of Essex, then truly you will know what it is to meet the devil! Besides, right now, the good friars of Godstone are probably singing the office of matins. Their holiness will protect us."

The monks were a long way off. Will doubted that their prayers could reach into the black depths of the king's forest. But Peter of Redvers was riding forward, and Will had no choice but to follow.

As they rode through the still night, Will felt the presence of the unhallowed spirits all around them. He made the sign of the cross and whispered prayers to St. Christopher and the holy Virgin.

"Your prayers won't save you, Little Rabbit," said d'Artois. He started to laugh again but his wounds must have pained him, for soon he was cursing softly. And then he was silent.

They rode on without talking. Will was sure he saw wraiths and demons twisted in the black branches. But at last the forest began to thin and the world became more gray than black. Soon they were back on the King's Road. And finally they came to Godstone.

The bells were ringing for prime, and the sky was a warm rosy glow in the east. Will had never, ever been so glad to see the day.

The gatekeeper admitted them, and as soon as the morning prayers were finished they were led through the cloister into the abbot's study.

Bernard, abbot of Godstone, was cousin to Sir John Belet. He looked a little like Will's father and had the same serious, calm demeanor. Once he heard their story, he ordered the prior to hide their treasures in the Chapter House. He had the horses stabled and fed, and d'Artois was sent to the infirmary. Then he had breakfast brought to his rooms for Will and Peter of Redvers.

"I must get to Woldingham at once," said Peter. "Sir John will be needing more men."

"But the road will not be safe for a lone knight wearing Sir John Belet's colors."

"True. I do not fancy another encounter with Essex's men."

"I think a disguise is in order," said the abbot. "A friar traveling on my business will be a good deal safer."

"I submit to the cowl," said Peter. "But not the tonsure."

"The cowl can be pulled over your head to hide your hair."

"What about Will?"

The abbot turned to Will and spoke kindly. "The cloister will hide you in case the earl of Essex comes."

Will bowed his head. Boys had little choice in their fate.

"You can work on your schooling, Master Will," said Peter. "And get a taste of the rule."

Will had no desire for a taste of the Benedictine rule. The school room and the cloister were *not* the realms of knighthood. The noble knight, Roland, would not let himself be becalmed in a cloister. Besides, how could he study anything while Blindley Heath was in such danger?

"Holy Father," he said.

"Yes, lad?"

"Could you find out how fares my family?"

"I will send a rider to Blindley Heath this morning and we shall have news by nones."

"Thank you," said Will.

The abbot smiled at Will. "Do not worry. Your good father won't let harm come to Blindley Heath."

Will hoped with all his heart it was true.

"Look after d'Artois," said Peter. "Watch how the monks doctor, and learn what you can. Remember what I said about second sons."

Will would remember.

He said good-bye to Peter and was taken down a long corridor to the novice master, Brother Paul.

What if a tonsure was to be part of his disguise? How could he present himself to the earl of Oxford with his head shaved?

He was brought to a low room lined with benches where a score of boys were bent over wooden shingles, their fingers grimy from the charcoal sticks they held. The lay brother introduced Will to Brother Paul and took his leave.

"Master Will," said Brother Paul. "Do you have any Latin?"

"A little, sir," said Will.

The boys were eyeing Will.

"How little?" asked Brother Paul, in Latin.

"My mother taught me the Psalms," said Will.

"That shall put you way ahead of these donkeys."

The boys laughed and Brother Paul smiled.

"Simon, take Master William Belet to the cellarer and ask Brother Ignatius to fit him out with a robe."

"Yes, sir!"

A small, dark-haired boy leapt to his feet and came to Will.

"Make sure the robe is not too long. And, Simon, hasten to return!"

"Yes, sir!"

Simon grabbed Will's hand and led him out to a long corridor.

"Are you the son of Sir John Belet of Blindley Heath?" he whispered.

Will nodded.

"My father has often spoken of Sir John," said Simon, still whispering. "Are you a new oblate? Did your mother really teach you Latin? Why didn't your parents stay to see you robed?"

"Well," said Will. "I'm sort of —"

"Shhh!" Simon held a finger to his mouth. "We aren't supposed to talk. So what are you doing here?"

They had crossed the cloister to another building, where Simon led Will through many twists and turns back out to the sunlit yard. All the while, Simon bombarded Will with questions. But Will had some questions of his own.

"Who is *your* father?" he whispered.

"Sir Brian Fitz Count of Wallingford," said Simon.

"Sir Brian!" said Will. "I've often heard *my* father praise him. Didn't they serve as pages together in Somerset?"

Simon nodded. "And they earned their spurs together, battling the border Scots. I'm glad we have met, Will Belet."

"I'm glad, too," said Will. "But why are you here?"

"I'm an oblate," said Simon.

"What *is* an oblate?" Will whispered.

"I have two older brothers, so my parents gave me to serve God."

Will nodded.

"I go to serve my uncle, the earl of Oxford," he said.

"Then why are you here?"

"We were attacked by some knaves of Essex while we were hunting."

"You were hunting with the men?" Simon's dark eyes grew round.

"In the king's forest," said Will.

"Shhh!" hissed Simon.

An ancient monk was shuffling toward them on old, unsteady legs.

"*Benedicite,*" said Simon.

"*Benedicite,*" said the monk. "You shall have a long penance if you continue chattering like a magpie."

Simon bowed his head and walked quickly away. He kept quiet long enough for Will to have more of a chance to look around.

Buildings surrounded the courtyard almost like the manor walls of Blindley Heath enclosing the bailey. But Godstone was larger and looked more like a prosperous village. A beautiful church dwarfed all the other buildings, its steeple soaring to the heavens. Friars, lay brothers, and serfs were hard at work in the yard. This, too, was like the manor, except there were no women, and most of the men wore long robes and the tonsure. Most, but not all.

Simon looked right and left before pulling Will into a niche behind a blacksmith's stall.

"They say Brother Julian can hear the mice saying

grace in the millhouse," he said. "Now tell me, why are you here?"

Will explained as quickly as possible. And all the while Simon's eyes shone with excitement.

"You escaped from a battle *and* spent the night in the forest with the demons abroad?"

Will nodded.

"And the earl of Essex is warring with your father?"

"Well . . ."

"The earl of Essex is a fiend!" said Simon. "There are many in the hospice who shan't walk, or see, or talk ever again because of what the earl's men did to them."

Will shuddered.

"Do you think the earl of Essex will come here?"

"They say he does not fear the hand of God." Simon leaned in closer to Will. "They say he has burned churches!"

Will knew Simon wasn't trying to add to his worries, but he had. What would become of Blindley Heath? How could his family survive against a man who feared not God?

"What tales are you telling today, Master Simon?"

The smith stood smiling down on them, his white teeth gleaming in his soot-darkened face.

"This is my new friend," said Simon.

"Pleased to meet you." The smith bowed to Will. "Now get on with your business!"

Simon leapt away before the smith's mighty hand could cuff his ear.

"Good day to you, Sir Smith," said Simon, and he raced across the courtyard with Will in tow.

Brother Ignatius, the cellarer, was especially displeased to hear their request.

"A new robe!" he grumbled. "As if they grew on trees."

"And please, sir," said Simon. "Brother Paul asks that it not be too long."

"But boys grow!" said Brother Ignatius. "Robes should be long enough to last!"

Then he looked severely at Will.

"How old are you, boy?"

"Twelve, sir."

"*Twelve!*" Simon shouted.

The cellarer glared at him.

"True, you are a small one," said Brother Ignatius.

Will felt the blood rush to his face.

"Wait here, I shall find something appropriate." The cellarer went into the next room.

"You aren't any bigger than I am," said Simon. "And I won't be ten until Martinmas in November."

"I was sick with the pox," said Will. "Mother said it hindered my growth."

"You'll catch up," said Simon, and he smiled.

Will smiled, too. He'd never met anyone quite like Simon.

"Bend down," said Will.

"It's not a trick?"

"I just need to see something," said Will. "Please?"

Simon bowed down, revealing a full head of curly black hair.

"You're not tonsured," said Will.

"Of course not," said Simon. "Boys never are."

V.
The Good of England

The news from home was bad. Even though Sir John and his men had defeated Essex's knights on the Roman road, killing off half their attackers, he and two others were wounded. But they all had made it back to Blindley Heath. However, Essex then came with a much larger force to punish Sir John and besiege Blindley Heath.

"Blindley Heath won't be able to hold out against Essex," said Will.

"You worry too much," said Simon.

"Essex could build a siege tower," said Will. "And he has mangonels and a battering ram tipped with copper. Blindley Heath isn't built to withstand a siege."

"Nothing has happened yet. And my father says your father is the ablest knight in Christendom," said Simon. "Besides, Peter of Redvers will ride to Oxford to get help from your uncle once he's raised a levy in Surrey. Now leave off, and help me with this Latin declension."

Will helped Simon with his studies. He worked in the gardens with the other oblates. And he prayed with the whole community at each of the seven canonical hours throughout the day and night. Days passed, and he never ceased worrying. If only he were grown. If only he were a knight and could fight for his home.

He went to the infirmary in the afternoon while the other boys played with a pig's bladder in the court-yard. D'Artois had improved under the monk's care. He hobbled about on a crutch and was more foul-tempered than ever.

"Blast these walls and spare me another night from this purgatory of holiness!" said d'Artois. They were on their way to the abbot's chambers for supper ten days after they first arrived at Godstone.

"You know we're not supposed to speak," said Will.

"A warrior is not bound by the churchmen's rules," said d'Artois. "Though I see they suit you well, Little Rabbit. Perhaps *you* belong here."

"No more than you, Sir Hobble de Clump," said Will, and leapt back as d'Artois swung his crutch.

At the abbot's study, a lay brother brought in an ewer and basin for them to wash their hands. Others began arriving with dishes of food and table settings. Soon Abbot Bernard entered the room.

"*Benedicite*, Father," said Will.

"*Benedicite*, my son," said Abbot Bernard, signing the cross.

The abbot washed his hands and signaled the lay brothers to start serving the food.

"The news is not the best," said the abbot. "Yesterday Peter of Redvers rode to your uncle at Oxford. But we don't know how long it will take the earl to raise a levy to aid Sir John."

"How long might it take?" asked Will

"A few days . . . a week at most," said d'Artois. "Aubrey de Vere is very powerful and will not let his stepsister's family suffer."

A week. Much could happen in a week. And with the enmity Earl Aubrey felt toward John Belet, perhaps he wouldn't hurry.

The servants passed platters of porpoise pudding, salmon pie, and gingered carp. Those of the cloister did not eat meat, though one dish of pork had been prepared to honor Will and d'Artois. They shared a trencher, but each had his own knife and spoon and silver goblet for wine. Normally boys did not eat with their elders, but the abbot treated Will with especial favor by inviting him to his table.

The abbot said grace and nodded for them to begin. Will didn't feel very hungry. And it seemed wrong for him to eat while his family was in such danger.

"Master Will," said Abbot Bernard, "you won't help your family if you become ill."

"What I don't understand," said Will, when they were eating the last course of fresh fruits, "is why

Essex is free to wage war against the lords of England?"

"He is King Stephen's man," said the abbot. "And so he may attack any who support Empress Matilda."

"But so many favor the empress and her son," said Will.

The abbot sighed.

"More are content with King Stephen's reign of chaos. They grow strong and rich as England is despoiled."

Will thought of the tales of King Arthur and his knights who had fought and died for the good of England. What would they think of a barony so greedy it was destroying England?

The abbot took a sip of wine and continued.

"Unfortunately Lord Henry is still a boy and too young to fight for himself. Those who now defy Empress Matilda would likely bend the knee to a new King Henry. I've heard that the young lord is the very image of his grandfather."

Will tried to imagine a boy who'd be capable of curbing the greedy barons and bringing peace to England. Henry would have to be like King Arthur, himself.

The bells were ringing for compline.

"The hour has grown late," said the abbot.

"Thank you for the bounty of your table," said d'Artois, rising slowly and awkwardly from his seat.

Abbot Bernard called a servant to escort d'Artois to the infirmary. Will was about to leave with him, when the abbot held him back.

"Stay a moment, Master Will. I would have a word with you."

They sat down again at the table, now cleared of food and linens. The abbot helped himself to more wine and turned to Will.

"Are you happy here?"

"Yes, Father."

"Brother Paul tells me you are an apt student."

Will shrugged. Should he say something?

The abbot leaned back against his richly carved high-backed chair.

"We all serve in different ways," he said. "Some fight the enemy on a battlefield and some are more suited to fight the devil with prayer."

What was he saying?

"Master Will, you do not look like a fighter of battlefields. Perhaps you would consider staying on at Godstone?"

Will felt a chill go through him. Did the abbot think that Blindley Heath was doomed? That Will would *have* to stay at Godstone?

"My son, you are pale. There is no cause for alarm. You may go to the dormitory and consider what I've said. Brother Paul will be wondering where you are."

"Thank you, Father," said Will. He bowed his head

for the abbot's blessing, then hurried back to the dormitory.

Later, when the candles were snuffed and the boys were supposed to be sleeping, Simon crept to Will's bedside.

"Why did you look so green when you came back from the abbot's rooms?"

"The abbot thinks I should stay at Godstone."

"So do I," said Simon.

"He *thinks* Blindley Heath will fall to Essex and I will *have* to stay here!"

"Will, he thinks you are too clever and too small to be a knight, that you should be a monk. Listen!"

It was the soft shuffling sound of Brother Paul's approach. Simon slipped back to his own bed, and Will pulled the scratchy wool cover around his shoulders, feigning sleep.

Was Simon right? Or was Blindley Heath doomed? Will turned on the narrow cot. Was he too small to be a knight? All the knights in the harpers' tales were giants among men. At home, he'd often been teased about being the small one — the Little Rabbit — but Lady Alice said in time he would grow. Sir John was sending him to Oxford to train for knighthood. Could they both be wrong?

Will fell into a fitful sleep, burdened with dreams of thick green smoke and races never won. He woke to the midnight bells for matins. He got up with the other boys, pulled on his boots, and was ready to go to the church for midnight worship when Brother Paul rushed into the dormitory.

"Master Will," he said. "Go to the abbot's chambers at once. He has news!"

Will ran across the midnight stillness of the cloister to the abbot's chambers. He ran in spite of the rule and the stern looks of the monks on their way to chapel.

What news? Good? Bad? It must be very important for the abbot to call for him during the sacred hour. He took a deep breath before knocking on the abbot's door.

"*Deo Gratias,*" said the abbot. "Come in."

With Abbot Bernard was a messenger. It was Alan at-Water from Blindley Heath!

"It's good news, Will," said Abbot Bernard. "The earl of Oxford and all the other lords of Surrey have routed Essex and his knaves."

Will looked from Alan to the abbot to Alan. He heard the words but found it hard to believe.

"It's true, Will," said Alan, beaming at him. "Your family's safe."

"But how?" said Will. "Peter of Redvers went to Oxford only yesterday."

"Earl Aubrey had already left Oxford," said Alan. "In fact, he and his men were in Surrey when Peter met up with them."

"How did he know to come?" asked Will.

"The earl's spies sent him word of Essex's ambush in the king's forest and he readied his forces that afternoon," said the abbot. "Now let us hasten to the church to praise the Lord and give thanks."

Will followed the lay brothers' torches to the church, repeating to himself Alan at-Water's news.

It was over. Earl Aubrey had saved Blindley Heath. Perhaps he had made his peace with John Belet. They were safe. They were all safe.

He knelt in the candlelight before the cross and gave thanks.

Simon was fidgeting in his pew with the other oblates as lauds followed matins. On any other night, Will would have been next to him. Soon, Sir John would come for Will and he'd be on his way, again, to Oxford to train for the knighthood. He stole a look at the abbot. What if Abbot Bernard convinced Sir John to leave him at Godstone? Godstone was a place of peace and learning, and the monks were that much closer to the angels. But Will wanted the world even if it meant uncertainty, danger, and leaving Simon, his first real friend. He wanted to join his brother at Oxford. He wanted to grow quickly and fight for the empress, mayhap to serve Lord Henry. Will wanted his chance at being a noble knight, in spite of the abbot's good intentions.

Finally the service ended, and the monks filed out

of the church to go back to the dormitories. Abbot Bernard took Will aside.

"Your father will come today, after sext," he said. "Go to your bed now and rest."

"Yes, Father," said Will.

He wanted to ask questions, to know more of what had happened at Blindley Heath. But boys were told very little; he'd have to wait.

The next morning before prime, Will and Simon stood in the lavatory splashing themselves with water from the frigid basins.

"I told you not to worry," said Simon.

"Still, it seems a miracle," said Will, "that Essex is defeated and Blindley Heath is safe."

Simon was silent a moment, gazing at Will.

"I'm glad Essex wasn't attacking my family's demesne," he said. "Will you go to Wallingford to see my mother and father?"

"Yes," said Will. "If you wish."

"It's not far from Oxford Castle. I'll draw you a map during lessons. My parents will be glad to meet the son of John Belet, and to have news of me. My sister, Edith, is the last of us still at home. It must get tedious for her; she'll be grateful for some company."

After lessons, the abbot sent word for Will to prepare for his father's arrival. Sir John and the earl would continue on to Oxford after a feast held in their honor. Will went back to the dormitory. The abbot hadn't said whether he'd be going to Oxford, too. Well, he would not greet his father looking like an oblate. It might give Sir John ideas. He got his own clothes from the blanket chest where they'd been stored with leaves of rosemary and mint to freshen them and keep away fleas and moths. It felt good to put off the coarse woolen robe. His linen shirt and tunic were cool and silky against his skin. He pulled on his breeches, hose, and hooded woolen over-tunic. He was just fastening his girdle when Simon came in.

Neither the rule nor the vigilance of Brother Paul and Brother Julian could keep Simon in check. He moved throughout the monastery — a free spirit.

"Good!" he said, smiling at Will. "I've found you. Look!"

Simon had a sheet of parchment.

"But where did you get this?"

"I borrowed it from the scriptorium," said Simon. "Don't look so worried. The scribblers will never miss it."

Simon had made a map showing Oxford Castle, Wallingford Castle, and everything of interest in between. Carefully drawn with blue-black ink were rivers, stands of trees, tiny cows and sheep grazing in fields, clusters of cottages, and three parish churches. There were also likenesses of Sir Brian Fitz Count, Lady Margaret, and Edith — Simon's father, mother, and sister.

"It's good," said Will. "It's *really* good. Abbot Bernard will have you in the scriptorium illuminating manuscripts before long."

"Not soon enough," said Simon, grinning.

He went to his bed and got something swaddled in cloth from under the pillow.

"The great knights carry relics in their sword hilts to keep them safe," said Simon. "This is for you."

Will unwrapped the cloth. It was a small cross of cherry, carved and polished to a rosy gleam.

"It is the finest thing I've ever had," said Will.

"Think of me when you are in the world doing great deeds," said Simon.

"Pray for me," said Will, "that I may!"

The bells for sext rang as Earl Aubrey de Vere, Sir John Belet, and their knights rode into Godstone. The monks lined the courtyard to greet them. Will and Ranulf d'Artois stood beside the abbot, who was richly dressed in damask and vair. Sir John stiffly dismounted his charger and winced when the horse nudged his shoulder. There was a gash on his brow and his left eye was swollen shut.

"Will," said Sir John. "Are you not happy to see me?"

"Oh, Father!" Will hastened to his side, glad to feel his strong embrace.

"Your eye," said Will. "Is it — ?"

"It will mend," said Sir John.

The earl had dismounted and was standing before the abbot. He surveyed the walls and towers of Godstone as Abbot Bernard spoke words of welcome. Will's uncle was at least a head above John Belet and the abbot, and seemed even taller, he stood so straight and still. His skin was very white and smooth, like polished stone. His cheeks were clean-shaven, but his upper lip was framed with bristles the color of granite.

"And this is Will," said Sir John, presenting him to the earl.

Will knelt before the earl's flickering glance and shuddered, chilled by the great man who would be his lord.

Soon Abbot Bernard was leading them all into the chapel for the singing of sext. And it wasn't until later, when they were seated at the high table, that Sir John and Will had a chance to speak at length.

"Father, please tell me of the battle at Blindley Heath."

Sir John leaned in closer, speaking quietly.

"It went badly for two days," he said. "I think the lords of Surrey may well have regretted aiding Blindley Heath against Essex. But when Earl Aubrey arrived yesterday noon with his great levy the battle quickly changed. Essex and his men soon departed."

"What damage?" asked Will.

Sir John took his hand.

"I have lost three good men. And half the village

was burned to the ground. But the parish church was saved, and for that we give thanks. The steward shall have it all put to rights by Christmas. No one will lack shelter."

Sir John took good care of the villagers and all who served Blindley Heath. He would not let any want for food or shelter. But Will could tell from his worried look that *many* had suffered, and it would take some doing to put all to rights.

"And you, my son," said Sir John, his face brightening. "The cloister has suited you; you look well cared for."

"The abbot has been very kind," said Will.

"Will would be a credit to Godstone," said Abbot Bernard. "What do you think of his staying on?"

This was what Will had been dreading.

"He certainly doesn't look a likely candidate for knighthood," said the earl, eyeing Will with his steely gaze.

Ranulf d'Artois for once kept his peace. There was an icy silence at the high table.

"Ha!" Sir John laughed and slapped the table. "True enough! Will is yet a slip of a lad. Time will cure that, brother."

Sir John put his hand on Will's and spoke gravely.

"Peter of Redvers tells me that this little rabbit kept his head during his first battle. Did he not save your leg, Sir Ranulf?"

D'Artois nodded.

"There are plenty of likely lads who've quailed at their first sight of blood," said Sir John. "One day Will shall win great honor as a knight."

Will was filled with gratitude. He dared not take his eyes off the table lest he betray his father's trust. But Sir John didn't know he'd nearly swooned at the ambush, nor did he know how Will had sickened at the bloodshed. Ranulf d'Artois knew. Will felt his eyes boring into him.

But perhaps Will could become the kind of knight he had dreamed of being. He'd give his immortal soul for the chance to try.

"What say you, Master Will?" asked Sir John. "Would you remain at Godstone?"

"No, my lord," said Will. "I would be a knight worthy of King Arthur and fight for the good of England."

Sir John grinned and squeezed Will's shoulder. But his eyes had a worried look. The earl of Oxford glared at Will, and his eyes were hard and cold as stone.

VI.
London Town

"Little Rabbit," said d'Artois as they rode side by side out of Godstone, "you have made an enemy where you might have made a friend."

"I don't understand."

"You had a precious opportunity to flatter your new lord. Instead you insulted him."

"I did what?" said Will. He hadn't said one word to his uncle.

"You said you would be a knight worthy of King Arthur," said d'Artois.

"But surely my uncle would find nothing to offend him in that," said Will.

"As you are now to be part of his household, he would have your *complete* loyalty," said d'Artois. "You should have said, you would be a knight worthy of your uncle the earl. And furthermore, talk of the good of England may not sound sweetly in your uncle's ears. To him it smatters of clerics' talk. Earl Aubrey de Vere cares not for lessons in righteousness. He will go his own way."

"But my uncle is one of Empress Matilda's strongest supporters," said Will. "Surely he believes in the good of England?"

D'Artois shook his head and eyed Will gravely. For once he didn't seem to be teasing.

"There is much for a rabbit to learn in the world," he said. "Be careful lest your tongue betray you."

Will nodded. He still didn't understand quite what he'd said wrong. But in the future he'd be more careful about revealing the matters of his heart.

Before leaving Godstone Will had written to his lady mother, giving thanks for her well-being and telling her of his stay with the monks and his meeting Simon Fitz Count. Sir John sent the letter back to Blindley Heath with his own awkwardly scrawled signature as his message to Lady Alice. Now Will wondered if he'd written anything that could give offense if Oxford eyes were to read the letter.

The journey to Oxford was filled with many marvels. Will felt he was finally on the road to his great adventure. All the new sights and sensations made him dizzy. There were so many things to see, so many things he wished to share with Simon. Will kept the cherry cross tucked under his cloak along with the wrapped honeycomb. Now and again he touched its satiny wood. When he got to Oxford, he might write down his impressions and send them to Godstone as well as to Blindley Heath. Perhaps he would first share his thoughts with John. Having an older brother at Oxford was going to be good.

London town was the most wonderful of all. It was surrounded by a great, high wall that had seven double gates and many towers like a castle beyond Will's imagining. Inside the walls, so many houses, people, and beasts were crowded together that Will wondered why the town wall didn't burst from trying to hold it all in. Most of the streets were quite narrow, lined with houses whose second stories jutted out over the street, nearly meeting the house opposite. D'Artois said that once a year the sheriff's man rode through the streets carrying a spear sideways above his head to make sure there was at least that much space left between the buildings.

Craftsmen worked in shops open to the street, hung with brightly colored signs showing what work they did. There were scissors for tailors, gloves for glovers, hides for leather workers, and anvils for ironmongers. In the squares were more shops and stands for traders in spices, silks, and damasks brought from the East. They shouted out their wares but could barely be heard above the clatter of horses and the shrill bargaining of housewives. Wherever there was an open space, jugglers, acrobats, minstrels, even dancing bears performed. Noblewomen stopped their gilded litters to watch, as did pilgrims, students, and clerks. Will wanted to watch too, but they rode on to Earl Aubrey's London house.

"At least we won't be struck in some verminous inn with thieves and murderers for bedfellows," said d'Artois.

So far they had stayed at two monasteries, and Will had been looking forward to an inn. He wouldn't have minded some bugs if it gave him a chance to hear the stories of merchants and traders who'd been to the ends of the earth.

Once they got to the earl's house and the horses were stabled, Will was sent off with five of the servants and two of the earl's knights to the public cookshop on the Thames.

Walking through London wasn't nearly as fine as riding. Down the center of each street ran a gutter where rubbish was thrown, including dead animals and the contents of slop jars. The people of means carried pomanders filled with sweet herbs to blot out the stench of the streets.

Will had never seen anything like the River Thames. On it sailed all kinds of boats and barges. Far down the wharves, he could see the bristling masts of merchant ships. On the riverfront were barges loaded with casks, from which men sold wine and ale to go with the food from the cookshops. The cookshops were vast kitchens on the riverbank where all types of meat were roasted, boiled, or baked in pastries. And sweets and sculptures of sugar and marzipan were made for the rich.

The servants busied themselves ordering dinner for Earl Aubrey and all his men. Will went to the river's edge to toss pebbles and watch the river traffic. The two knights sat behind him on the bank, talking quietly, but loud enough for Will to hear.

"I shall be glad to get back to my manor and my wife."

"And I, as well."

"I wonder that Sir John leaves his sons with his brother-in-law. If I had a demesne the earl coveted, I wouldn't give him my only sons."

"Sir John is no fool. He will make some arrangement to protect the boys."

"Look you, the servants have ready our dinner. It is time to go back."

"Master Will!"

"Aye," said Will and followed after them, wondering if he could believe his own ears. The knights had implied that his uncle was contemplating something evil. Yet he had just ridden to the aid of the Belets. The knights must be mistaken.

On the way back to the earl's London house, beggars, smelling the good food, came out in droves. They held up misshapen limbs and pleaded for morsels or coins. They wore filthy rags over flesh covered with running sores. Will pulled away from their grasping hands as he wished he could pull himself away from the memory of the conversation of the two knights. It was even more sickening than the beggars.

The knights had to be wrong. Even if the earl still bore ill will toward Sir John, he would never harm the sons of Lady Alice. Will wished there was someone he could talk to, if only to assure himself their words meant nothing. Simon would have an answer and he could trust Simon with this story. But he dared not repeat a word of such slanderous gossip to anyone, nor commit it to writing. Maybe, once he got to Oxford, his brother John could discredit the story.

Later, when they sat at the earl's high table eating their dinner, Will studied his uncle as much as he could without calling attention to himself. The earl spoke only when asked a direct question, and even then he seemed displeased. Will's father talked with all the knights, encouraging them to tell about their manors and families or their deeds in battle. There was much talking and laughter at the table except at the very center, where sat Earl Aubrey. And that was a cold, silent place.

But it was no crime for the earl to distance himself from the others. Earl Aubrey de Vere had every right to be haughty. Wasn't he a great lord with vast estates throughout England? The knights had said he coveted Blindley Heath. That couldn't be true. There was no sense to it.

"My good brother —" said Sir John to the earl.

Will thought he saw the earl wince at being called brother. Or perhaps he was merely nodding his head.

"I would ask a boon," said Sir John.

"Ask it," said the earl.

"This young knight," Sir John said, putting his hand on Ranulf d'Artois's shoulder, "has served me well and in so doing suffered a grievous injury. He will need some time to heal. I would not have him moping around Blindley Heath with nothing to do."

The earl looked bored. But Sir John kept talking in the same friendly, unhurried way.

"Take him on at Oxford. Let him help train the pages."

Will nearly choked on a mouthful of pigeon pie. His father couldn't be serious! But he *was*. What's worse, so was the earl.

"This is not such a great thing to ask," he said. "Ranulf d'Artois may abide with me while he mends."

How could this be happening? Will felt stunned. If d'Artois was to help train the pages, Will's life in Oxford would be an absolute misery instead of a glorious road to honor.

"What say you, Will?" asked Sir John. "It will be good to have a friendly face at Oxford, won't it?"

"Yes, sir," said Will, looking over at d'Artois's scowling black brow. A *friendly* face would be good.

It wasn't until they were setting out from London in the cold, shadowless hour before dawn that part of the knights' conversation came back to Will. They had said that Sir John would make some arrangement to protect the boys. Was d'Artois to be Will's protector?

Impossible!

VII.
Oxford Castle

They rode through the stockade into the outer bailey of Oxford Castle to sounds of trumpets and the cries of heralds. Pennants flew from the great tower and all the battlements. Servants and villeins came out to see the earl's return. On they rode past a myriad of workshops that lined the outer curtain wall. It was nearly as busy and crowded as London town.

Before them rose the turrets of the higher inner curtain wall and above them the honey-colored stone of the castle keep. The keep reached up to touch the sun and the fleecy clouds scudding by. It was as tall as the church spires of Godstone. Aubrey de Vere, earl of Oxford, could not possibly have designs on Blindley Heath, when he held this great castle. The knights Will had overheard on the riverbank in London must have been terribly mistaken.

"Master Will," said d'Artois. "You look like a country bumpkin. Stop gawking."

Will *felt* like a country bumpkin.

The outer bailey was a lush pasturage where cattle and sheep might thrive even during a siege. Most of the inner bailey was paved with cobblestones and swept clean of debris. A garden bloomed next to the south-facing wall. There were beds of vegetables, herbs, and flowers. Up against the wall, espaliered fruit trees were laden with pears, plums, and small red apples. The branches had been trained to grow in strange and beautiful patterns.

"It looks like the work of fairies," said Will.

"Flattened trees," said d'Artois. "Hmph!"

A beautiful lady entered the courtyard from the tower. She wore a cloak and gown of jewel-like colors, trimmed in snowy ermine. The ladies who accompanied her were also richly dressed, but none could match her fine beauty or grace.

"She looks like the queen of the fairies," said Will.

"The Lady Elaine is flesh and blood, just as those silly flat trees are wood, leaves, and fruit," said d'Artois.

"The Lady Elaine," breathed Will.

She came forward and curtsied to the earl.

"Welcome home, my lord," she said.

The earl stared down at her from the height of his great charger. Lady Elaine bore his gaze calmly, then turned to Sir John.

"And twice welcome to you, noble knight, brother-in-law and my father's cousin."

Sir John's shoulder was mending, and he leapt from his horse like a young knight, removed his gauntlet, and took the lady's white hand in his.

"I am most heartily glad to be once again in your lovely presence, little cousin."

"A pretty speech, good Sir John," said Lady Elaine. She lightly touched his injured brow. "I'm sorry to see you bearing the marks of your battles."

" 'Tis nothing, milady."

"Now, my good knight, show me the treasure you have brought me."

"Will," said Sir John. "Come and meet your new mistress."

Will climbed off his horse and knelt before the lady.

"Rise up, Master Will," she said, "that I may look on you."

Will stood, wishing his jerkin wasn't so stained and that his hands were cleaner.

"Sir John, you must be proud to have two such fine sons."

Lady Elaine caught hold of Will's sweaty hands with her cool, delicate fingers. Her brow was so fair, her eyes a deep blue tinged with violet. Even this close she was hardly real, more like one of the fairies. And she was tiny, barely taller than Will! His heart thudded against his jerkin — he'd never been so near such perfection.

"It is true, I shall be your mistress," she said. "I

would also be your friend. Welcome, Master Will."

"I . . . I . . ." Will felt as if his tongue were knotted. "Thank you, kind lady," he managed at last.

Hoofbeats sounded on the cobblestones. A young squire with blazing copper curls drew his horse up to the gathering and leapt nimbly to the ground.

"Son!" said Sir John, embracing the rider.

Will knew he was gawking but couldn't help it. This *grown man* was his brother John!

"Father!" John stepped back, eyeing Sir John's wound. "I hope you punished the knave who cut you."

"Aye," said Sir John. "That I did."

"Is Mother well? My sisters? And Blindley Heath?" asked John. "Did Essex do much damage?"

"Everyone is fine," said Sir John. "Essex was sent packing before he could cause much harm. Now, greet your brother."

John turned to Will and his face froze.

"Good lord!" he said. "He's not grown at all."

"John!" said his father.

Will felt his skin go clammy.

Lady Elaine laughed gently, squeezing Will's hands. Her laughter was like a cooing dove.

"Beware, Master John," she said, "lest one day, your little brother outstrips you!"

John flushed red.

"Surely my lady jests," he said.

"No, John," said Lady Elaine, her voice low and serious. "I speak true. And I say, beware."

Will shivered. Was Lady Elaine truly one of the fairy folk, able to see a man's destiny?

Meanwhile the earl had dismounted and was giving orders to vassals and grooms. He marched into the tower without one word of greeting to his beautiful wife. Must great men act so coldly to maintain their dignity? Will remembered the knights' talk by the river and shivered. Perhaps John would be able to answer his questions. But John had looked so disgusted when he saw his "little" brother, Will wondered whether he would be able to ask *anything* of John.

"Come," said Lady Elaine. "You shall have refreshments after your long journey."

Still holding Will's hand, she led them up the stone stairs of the tower of Oxford Castle to the most lavish room he had ever seen. Embroideries and carpets from the East covered the walls. The ceiling was deep blue, embellished with golden stars. The floor rushes had been plaited with wildflowers and herbs. Each step released a cloud of fresh scent.

Ewers and basins were brought in to wash away the dust of the journey. Will looked for a friendly face among the pages and servants but found only imitations of his uncle's cool disdain. The earl was nowhere in sight. And his knights had slipped away.

Lady Elaine poured out wine, while pages passed platters of cheese, fruit, and bread. The ladies assisted the pages and when all were served they perched on stools or on the great chest near the fireplace. Will sat next to his father on a stone bench carved from the wall. John and d'Artois paced around the room. D'Artois should have been resting his leg, thought Will, though perhaps he too felt nervous and awkward. John seemed angry, or impatient — maybe both.

Lady Elaine queried Sir John about the ambush in the king's forest and the battle. Now and again her attention shifted to Will, d'Artois, or John.

John seemed immune to her spell, but d'Artois's color rose as the lady asked after his wounds and praised his endurance. Will felt his face go scarlet when Sir John credited him with saving d'Artois's leg. Lady Elaine looked at him with true admiration in her blue eyes.

"Master Will," she said. "You are brave, indeed."

Will hoped that Lady Elaine would never know the fear in his heart.

"Lady Alice has the healer's art," said Sir John. "I'm glad Will's picked up some of it — that those extra years at home were not wasted."

"What else did your mother teach you, Will?" asked Lady Elaine. "Can you read and write?"

Will nodded. He cleared his throat and still his voice squeaked. "And I have a little Latin."

"I shall see that your studies are not neglected while you remain at Oxford Castle," said the lady, "in spite of my lord's contempt for learning." She looked quite fierce.

There was a moment's uncomfortable silence.

"Gentlemen," she said, changing back to the honey-toned fairy queen. "Perhaps you would see your quarters. John, your brother will want a tour of his new home. Make sure he meets Squire Wat and the other pages."

"Yes, milady," said John.

"Sir Ranulf," she said, "I beg you to repose yourself until the dinner hour."

D'Artois bowed and they all left the room, following John down the curved stone staircase back to the courtyard. Will felt as if he'd just walked out of a dream. The Lady Elaine was so beautiful *and* kind. Being stuck with d'Artois wouldn't matter so much as long as *she* was in Oxford Castle, too.

They left d'Artois in the small room off the great hall, which he would share with Sir John. Beds had been made up for them with fresh linens and brocade coverlets. At home, visiting knights had to make do with the benches in the great hall. Their squires usually slept on the rushes with the dogs.

Will was glad to spend some time alone with his father and John. If only John weren't so prickly. It nearly spoiled the adventure of exploring Oxford Castle. There were so many wonders. In the great hall a painted frieze of knights on horseback marched all around the walls in a brilliant procession. Above the frieze, the walls had been whitewashed and then painted in a pattern of red lines to look like stones. Within each "stone" was painted a different wild-flower. On the wall behind the earl's dais were hung gem-bright carpets from the East.

" 'Tis quite a sight," Sir John said to Will. "Isn't it?"

"Aye, sir, it's . . ." Will was at a loss.

Sir John laughed and clapped Will on the back.

"That it is, boy, that it is!"

After the great hall, John marched them in a circle around the courtyard, beginning with a honeycomb of rooms built into the curtain wall. Nearest the keep to the west were apartments for the steward, his staff, and noble guests. John hurried them past buildings attached to the inner curtain wall, farther from the stronghold, the barracks, stables, and the forge. The gatehouse, opposite the keep, was formed of two stout towers containing guard rooms and stores. Continuing their circular tour, they passed many workshops and the kitchens and came to the large chapel, snug against the east side of the keep. Will longed to linger in the chapel and other rooms fitted out for nobles. There he could see the exquisite white hand of Lady Elaine. The earl had built a castle more formidable than anything Will could have ever imagined. Lady Elaine graced it with beauty. To work such magic . . . perhaps she really was a fairy queen.

But John seemed interested only in the fortifications. He'd paused at the gatehouse only to point out its strengths at repelling invaders. It was then, when John was excited and happy, that Will could see traces of the brother he'd known at Blindley Heath, the brother he'd hoped to call "friend." Sir John nodded and looked with approval at all John described. Oxford Castle incorporated all the latest theories of castle defense brought back from the Holy Land by the Crusaders.

"The enemy might begin a siege," boasted John. "But they could never finish it. The castle is safe against all types of attack."

"Never say never," said Sir John, smiling grimly.

At last John brought them to the outer bailey by climbing a series of removable wooden stairs that ran along the stables, went up over the ramparts, and descended the other side into a large open yard. This was where the pages, squires, and young knights trained. One boy was tilting at the quintain, sitting atop a mechanical horse pulled by servants. Two boys were sparring with blunted short swords and others were loading crossbows and long bows and shooting at a target hung from the curtain wall.

A bull-like man, built low to the ground, was barking orders at everyone.

"Squire Wat," said John, "I'd like you to meet my father."

"Sir John," said the squire, bowing his head. "This is indeed an honor."

Will's father nudged him toward Squire Wat.

"I've brought you a new charge, Squire," said Sir John. "My second son, William Belet, known as Will."

The squire looked Will over with eyes shaded by a dark bristling brow that grew straight across his forehead.

"He seems a mite young," said Squire Wat.

"Not young," said Sir John. "His growth was held up by the pox. Will shall be thirteen by next first of May."

Squire Wat continued to stare darkly at Will, then turned to John.

"Take him 'round to the other boys, then show him his bunk," said the squire. "Sir John, it's been a pleasure, excuse me." And he strode over to the boys with swords and began berating their clumsiness.

John introduced Will to the boys. Grudgingly, each one stopped what he was doing to greet Will, then returned immediately to the task at hand. Gregory, Hugh, Charles, Edgar . . . It was a blur of names and faces. No boy had really looked at Will and not one smiled.

They climbed back over the wooden stairs to the stables and from there entered directly into the barracks. It wasn't much different from the dormitory at Godstone, except there were fewer crosses. As at Godstone, there was a separate room for the boys.

"Get yourself settled," said Sir John, "and put on a

clean tunic and hose for dinner. I would have a word with your brother."

Will climbed a rickety ladder to the boys' barracks and found his bow and quiver of arrows piled on a cot. His wooden chest, carved over with a pattern of holly leaves twining his initials, had been brought from Blindley Heath. Now it sat at the foot of his cot. He opened it and found a clean tunic, shirt, and hose. The sealed bundle containing the honeycomb was beneath the hose. Will held the comb a moment before replacing it in the chest. He'd come such a long way from Blindley Heath. He'd waited so many years for this, to be in the world of men. And now he saw how much further he must go along the road to knighthood. His brother's angry voice rose from the floor below and roused him from his daydreams.

"How can you be serious about this?" said John.

"Now, now, he'll come along," said Sir John. "Size isn't everything."

"But surely you can't mean to have him knighted?" John's voice grew louder. "Will is practically a dwarf!"

"Enough!" His father spoke quietly, but it silenced John. "He will do fine. It is your duty to help him find his way. If I hear otherwise, you shall have to answer to me."

"Yes, sir," said John, his voice still hot with anger.

"Will," called his father.

"Sir," said Will, leaning over the ladder opening.

"John will bring you to the great hall for dinner."

Will nodded. He quickly changed his clothes and climbed down the ladder to John. He couldn't look at his brother. He could barely breathe.

"Just having you here will be embarrassment enough," said John. "Try not to make it worse!"

Why should John hate his own brother so much? Was this what he had learned at Oxford Castle?

Will dug his nails into the palms of his hands until the pain muted John's stinging words. God willing he'd not be an embarrassment to anyone. God willing.

VIII.
Accident?

The morning after Sir John left for Blindley Heath, Will began his life as a page. Even with his father's presence to shield him, it was clear Oxford Castle did not welcome Will Belet. Now Will was on his own. Only Lady Elaine softened the harshness. But her influence in the castle was very limited.

"*Get up!*" Squire Wat shouted Will out of slumber. Then grabbing Will's ear, he pulled him out of bed. It was way before dawn and cold as death in the barracks. The other boys were already up and dressed. Will hurried into the earl's uniform, colored azur and argent, that hung on him like a great sack.

"Empty the piss pots into the cesspit at the end of the stables," barked the squire. "Then scour them with sand and lime."

He handed Will a long-handled brush and a pot of quicklime.

"Don't stand there collecting lint!" he shouted. "*Hop to it!*"

Will stumbled down the ladder, holding the foul pots as far from his nose as possible. The men's barracks were empty. John and the other young squires had gone hunting, so John was spared the sight of Will performing this lowly task. Perhaps this was just the sort of embarrassment John dreaded. But what could Will do, except obey orders?

"The new page always gets the piss pots," said a villein working at the cesspit, covering the ordure with lime and soil. "Squat Wat thinks this is the way to let you know he's the boss."

"Squat Wat!" said Will. "That's a good one."

"Well, don't let *him* hear it."

Will smiled and that got him through it. Once the pots were cleaned and inspected by Squat Wat, he was sent to the kitchens.

Giselle the cook harried the boys through a scant breakfast of stale bread and ale. Then she sent them with trays holding daintier fare to serve apartments in the castle keep. Will was stuck with the nursery tray. Gregory, who was serving Lady Elaine, grudgingly showed him the way. The children, their nurses, and lesser lady attendants slept in a large room beyond Lady Elaine's apartments. A steep, narrow, wooden stair at the far side of the great hall led past the earl's apartments directly to the nursery. Will's tray was heavy with covered bowls of warm milk, flagons of wine, and soft warm loaves of bread swathed in linen wraps. There were even small pots of honey.

Will's stomach churned. The comforting smells of the nursery food were so at odds with his own breakfast. It was maddening to watch the little ones dawdle with food he would have devoured.

The door opened and Lady Elaine appeared, her long hair in loose plaits, silvery against the blue morning robe.

"Mother!" The children raced to her. She was so delicate, surely they would topple her.

"My little ducks," she said, reaching out to pet each child. "Are you being very good?"

"Oliver pinched me," said Bertrade.

Lady Elaine looked severely at Oliver, which brought on hot tears and an apology.

"You must all be sweet with each other," said Lady Elaine, hugging her son.

"Good morrow, Master Will," said the lady. "How do you fare this morning?"

Will could only smile and bow, afraid to risk speech.

"Dame Catherine, could you fix this lad's tunic? It does not do him justice."

A stout lady all in green eyed Will critically.

"It will be but a few stitches, milady."

"Master Will, oblige Dame Catherine by removing your tunic," said Lady Elaine.

Will felt the blood rush to his face. He couldn't disobey, neither could he remove anything in front of *her*.

"Come to the wardrobe, lad," said the dame. "You shall have a bit of privacy."

As she sewed, Dame Catherine besieged Will with questions about Lady Alice and his journey from Blindley Heath. Will was happier listening to her prattle about the goodness of her mistress, Lady Elaine. By the time Dame Catherine finished stitching his tunic so that it fit neatly about his shoulders and didn't hang so long below his knees, the children had finished their breakfast and Lady Elaine had retired to her chambers. Will gathered up the dishes and made haste to the kitchens.

Giselle greeted him with a box on the ears.

"That will teach you to loiter on the stairs!" she said. "Now get you to the yard!"

Will ran as fast as he could, but the pages were already lined up at attention, facing Squire Wat and Ranulf d'Artois. Will slipped behind Hubert, who was tall and broad and provided good cover.

"New page to the front!" shouted Squire Wat.

Will moved to Hubert's side. He stood as tall and straight as he could. No matter how he felt inside, he'd at least try to look brave.

"There are no excuses for tardiness!" said Squire Wat. "Report to the stables after the dinner hour."

Will nodded.

Squire Wat stepped forward and slapped Will's face.

"*Sir!* You say, '*Yes sir!*' "

"*Yes sir!*" said Will, his face smarting.

D'Artois looked on coldly. Was he enjoying this? No one at Blindley Heath would have hit Will.

They started with the long bow, shooting at targets set up along the outer curtain wall. By now the sun was well up and warming the yard. Will's skill with the bow had not deserted him. Arrow after arrow found its mark. He was doing something right for the first time since his arrival at Oxford Castle.

"Look, you dolts and oafs!" bellowed Squire Wat, standing directly behind Will. "This puny brat is out-shooting the lot of you!"

Puny brat! Will seethed. His next arrow glanced off the target and dropped to the ground.

"Temper, temper, Little Rabbit," said d'Artois. "A knight must learn control."

"Little Rabbit!" The squire hooted. "Isn't he just, pink nose and all!"

The boys around Will snickered. This was what he'd dreaded most from d'Artois. He'd hoped that at Oxford Castle he'd be known as Will, Page, even Oaf or Dolt, anything but Little Rabbit. But from now on Will would be cursed with his nursery name.

Will wiped his sweaty hand on his tunic to prepare another arrow and felt Simon's cross tucked inside his girdle. It steadied him. He wasn't going to let d'Artois, Squat Wat, or Little Rabbit get in his way. He would become a knight worthy of King Arthur, in spite of it all. He drew an arrow, aimed, and struck the bull's eye.

"That's better," said d'Artois, and moved along to deplore Godfrey's posture.

The broad sword gave Will much more trouble than the bow. First of all, he could barely lift it. The swords were real, though well blunted, and the tips were capped. The boys wore heavy padding so no one would be cut. Even so, getting hit by the sword was no joke.

Will was paired with Hubert, who loomed monstrous above him. The only advantage Will had was speed, which he used to dodge the blows that rained down on him. Half the time he could do little with his own sword but drag it behind him on the ground.

Before long, Will realized that Squire Wat, d'Artois, and all the other pages had gathered round and were having a good laugh at his expense. That is, all except d'Artois were laughing. At least John wasn't around to witness this.

"Will Belet," said d'Artois, his voice cold as steel. "Stand your ground and fight!"

Will stopped in his tracks. Squat Wat had paired him with Hubert just to provide this show, just to see Will look ridiculous. It made him furious. And his rage gave him the strength to lift the sword and deal Hubert such a blow he went sprawling on the ground.

"You aimed too low," said d'Artois. "And hesitated too long."

"Yes, sir," said Will, without meeting his eye.

Squire Wat wiped the tears of laughter from his face and approached Will.

"That's enough for you today," he said. "Get you to the buttery to learn your table duties."

"*Yes, sir!*" said Will and started off before realizing he hadn't the faintest idea of how to find the butler's closet.

"Please, sir," he said, turning back. "Where is the buttery?"

"*Botheration!*" said the squire. "*Godfrey!* Take Rabbit to Alfred the butler and make sure he learns the way! *Make haste!*"

"*Sir!*"

Godfrey flew past Will, up the wooden stairs, and over the battlements. Will scrambled after him with all the boys in the yard laughing loudly.

Will and Godfrey were just crossing the inner bailey when the huntsmen came thundering through the gatehouse into the yard.

Will stopped dead in his tracks. His brother, John, was draped across a bay horse, his body limp. An arrow shaft stuck out from his back and his jerkin was soaked in blood.

The men were off their horses and shouting to servants who came running.

"Get a litter!"

"Send for the barber!"

"Hurry up, scum!"

"Bring him to Lady Elaine!"

John was lifted from the horse onto a litter and carried to the tower.

"Hunting accident," said Godfrey. He didn't sound the least bit alarmed or surprised.

But Will was nearly too stunned to move. Was John dead or alive? What had happened? Whatever, he must help. He raced after the men and up the stairs to Lady Elaine's chamber.

Already, Dame Catherine was cutting away John's jerkin and tunic to expose the wound. Lady Elaine was ordering the men and her ladies.

"Get my medicines! Bring bandages! Quickly! We must stop the bleeding!"

The barber arrived, carrying a bag of tools and his basin. He doused the wound with spirits, then had two men hold John steady while he cut the flesh and eased out the barbed arrowhead. John groaned horribly.

He lived! But the wound looked bad, and there was too much blood.

"Will!"

Noticing him, Lady Elaine beckoned him near.

"Have you seen Lady Alice treat such a mishap?"

"Aye, milady."

"Then stay and help."

She sent the others out of her chambers, and they set to work to save John Belet.

The arrow had been slowed by John's thick leather jerkin, and still the wound was deep. He had been hit at fairly close range.

Dame Catherine sat close to John, giving him sips of spirits, mopping his brow and speaking words of comfort, as if to a babe. John was grown, nearly a knight, but Will could tell even without seeing his face that John was crying.

Inside, Will was quaking. He, too, felt like crying. But his hands held steady. He helped as Lady Elaine and the barber cleaned the wound and stanched the bleeding. The barber gave instructions and Will prepared a poultice. The barber and Will bandaged John while Lady Elaine prepared a sleeping draught.

"Thank you, Barber," said Lady Elaine. "My young squire has been well attended."

"It helps to have such able assistants," said Barber.

Lady Elaine took Will's stone-cold hand in hers.

"Will John be all right?" whispered Will.

Lady Elaine led them to a far corner.

"What think you, Barber?"

"He has a fair chance," said Barber. "I think the shaft was stopped by muscle and bone. His vital organs were spared."

"We must trust in God," said Lady Elaine.

"Yes, milady, it is in His hands."

"What deed is this?" said d'Artois, coming into the room.

"It is a hunting accident," said Lady Elaine. "Yet *another* accident at Oxford Castle."

"Were there witnesses?" asked d'Artois.

"Of course not!" said Lady Elaine.

Her voice was cold with anger and her beautiful face was set in hard lines. What were they saying? What *had* happened to John? Was this the prophecy of the knights in London Town? Was this the earl's doing?

IX.
The Nursery

The accident rearranged Will's life at Oxford Castle. Both John and Will were installed in the nursery.

"You cannot keep me with the women and babes!" said John.

"Yes, I can," said Lady Elaine. "You will stay here until Barber and I give you leave to return to the barracks."

"The earl will not stand for it!"

"Your recovery is *my* responsibility," said Lady Elaine. "And I would have you near."

"Milady," said Will, "couldn't I sleep in the barracks?"

"Will, I need you here to look after your brother. My ladies cannot nurse him and mind the children." Lady Elaine's eyes bore into him. How could he refuse her anything?

"Yes, milady," said Will.

Very little was said about the accident. Such snippets as Will heard made it seem quite an ordinary event.

"These things happen."

"No one's to blame."

The earl had said nothing as far as Will knew. In the four days since the accident, he'd not bothered to come see John. But perhaps it would be too unseemly for the mighty lord to enter the nursery. Sir John had often played with his children, even the little girls. But Will's father didn't have all of Oxfordshire and the northern marches in his care. Other than the ladies, John's only visitor was d'Artois. He came every day, dragging his bad leg up the stairs. He'd perch on a chest and, mostly scowling, talk to John about hunts and battles.

Will wanted to believe it *was* an accident. But then he'd remember the look on d'Artois's face, and the tone of Lady Elaine's voice when she had said "Yet *another* accident." John was lucky. The wound was clean and not festering. The arrow *had* been slowed by his jerkin and stopped by a rib. The rib had cracked, but not splintered. The barber said he would heal. Will wondered if John's survival was the real accident.

Will's training in the yard went slowly, and Squat Wat had many a laugh at Will's expense. D'Artois continued to find fault with his every move. The squire's jibes only served to humiliate or anger Will, but under d'Artois's critical scrutiny, his skills improved. D'Artois could point out precisely where he went wrong, whether it was aiming his arrow, tilting at the quintain, or even hefting the impossible broadsword. On the next try, Will was able to earn a satisfied grunt from d'Artois. He was learning the knightly skills even if he was a little rabbit.

At the dinner hour he was sent to Alfred the butler who taught him to serve as cupbearer to Lady Elaine. The rest of the time he was stuck in the nursery with John and the children.

John was a terrible patient. He complained and raged and would not be still in spite of his pain. Twice he'd reopened the wound, which led to fevers that Will and Lady Elaine fought with potions. It fell to Will to calm and distract John, so that the wound might have a chance to heal.

Lady Elaine helped by supplying them with a precious book scribed and illumined by the monks of the Priory of Osney. It was a collection of wondrous tales called *The History of the Kings of Britain*. Will read it aloud, translating the Latin as he went. It had stories of valiant kings and their mighty deeds. Everyone, even John, liked the tales of King Arthur best — they told of a dark and desperate time. But when Arthur ruled England all the barons of the realm fought to preserve their land and protect the weak and helpless. Now the barons fought not for glory but for greed, and all of England suffered.

"Little brother," said John, "you will never be a knight. But well you read their tales."

Fortunately John slept a great deal. Will suspected that Lady Elaine laced his medicine with sleeping draughts. While John slept Will was at the mercy of the children. There were six girls and two boys. Only Oliver, Anne, and Gwyneth were Lady Elaine's children. The other children were orphaned nobles in the earl's care until they were old enough to inherit their titles. The earl's eldest son from his first marriage was already a young knight attending Empress Matilda.

"Tell us again about King Arthur," Gwyneth teased.

"Tell the part where he cuts the Saxon lords to pieces," said Harold.

"No," said Oliver. "Tell about when he cuts the Gauls to pieces."

Will couldn't believe he had come so far only to find himself back in the nursery. The last fortnight had seemed an eternity.

"Will," said Dame Catherine one morning, "go to milady's chamber and fetch my spindle."

Will went through the closet that separated Lady Elaine's chamber from the nursery and was about to enter the room when he was stopped by the sound of Lady Elaine's voice.

"I've done all that I could," she said, "short of sending them both back to Blindley Heath."

"Forgive me, milady," said d'Artois. "I am only angry with myself for failing my lord."

"You could not have prevented the mishap," said Lady Elaine. "But now we can use it to our advantage. You and I will work together."

"You can't keep them in the nursery forever," said d'Artois.

"It need not be forever," said Lady Elaine. "Only long enough for us to make other arrangements."

D'Artois walked toward the open closet. Will quickly turned and went back to the nursery.

"Well," said Dame Catherine, "where's my spindle?"

"Sorry," said Will. "I couldn't find it."

"Bother!" said Dame Catherine. "I suppose I must look it out myself."

What were Lady Elaine and d'Artois plotting? Boys were never told anything. But John was old enough to have some say, especially if they were thinking of sending them back to Blindley Heath.

Will had to wait until after supper, when the children had been put to bed and the ladies were attending Lady Elaine, before he could talk with John. He'd held back John's medicine so he wouldn't fall asleep.

"Why do you think we've been kept in the nursery?" asked Will.

For the first time since he'd arrived in Oxford John looked at him as if he were a person and not an insect.

"I don't know," he said. "Do you?"

Will shrugged.

"What if it wasn't an accident?"

"Don't be a dolt," said John. "Hunting mishaps happen all the time."

"They don't at Blindley Heath," said Will.

"Well, they do here," said John.

"They do?"

"Yes," said John. He looked at Will and a shiver seemed to run through him. "What makes you ask?"

Will looked around to make sure the children slept and the ladies were still out of the room.

"I heard Lord Aubrey's knights say that he coveted Blindley Heath and meant to get rid of us," he whispered.

"Ridiculous!" said John. "The earl may not be a great friend to our father, but that doesn't mean he'd take Blindley Heath. Besides, he has Oxford and all the north border demesnes."

"It doesn't make sense to me, either," said Will. "But I think d'Artois is here to protect us."

"Well, a fat lot of good *he's* done," said John.

"John, *could* the earl want Blindley Heath?"

"As small as it is, Blindley Heath has value," said John. He tapped his fingers on the coverlet, tried to turn on his side, and groaned.

"It would be a fine prize for the earl's youngest."

"Oliver?" said Will. "He's just a baby."

"Someday he'll be grown. Then he'll need his own

demesne. Blindley Heath would suit him well. And it would suit the earl, as the manor owes fealty to no one but the king."

It did make sense, after all. The earl's first-born son would have Oxford and all its holdings. His other children would have no part of it. Only that which the earl had bought or acquired in his lifetime could be left to them. Blindley Heath would be just the right-size holding for Oliver. And it would particularly suit the proud earl.

Blindley Heath. Blindley Heath was meant for John.

"Lady Elaine might send us back to Blindley Heath," said Will.

"She can't," said John. "Father wouldn't let her. It would only make things worse."

"How could they be worse?" said Will.

John gave him such a look. It would be worse if Blindley Heath were caught up in this. But the earl wouldn't hurt his stepsister. Would he?

"D'Artois won't tell me," said Will. "But you could find out what is going on."

"You think he'd tell me?"

"You're a man," said Will.

John laughed, then grimaced from the pain.

"Little brother," he said, smiling at Will, "you have much to learn."

Will sighed.

"Anyway, you seem to know a great deal without having been told anything. Keep your ears open and let me know what else you hear," said John. "And don't speak of this to anyone."

"Who would I tell it to?" asked Will. "None but the children will speak with me."

"That is how it is here," said John. "Friendship is not encouraged. Now give me my medicine. I would sleep."

The draughts insured John a sound sleep. Will was not so blessed. His nights were fraught with worries about John, Blindley Heath, and his own fate. It seemed much simpler in King Arthur's time. The road to knighthood was more straightforward. Could Will succeed? Could he become as valiant a knight as Sir Gawaine, with his own poor skills, and when the way was muddied with treachery?

During the day he tried to ignore his fears. But it was especially difficult to fulfill his pledge and write to Lady Alice. What could he tell her that wouldn't cause her alarm? He tried to make light of John's injury, stressing the skill of Lady Elaine and the barber and John's recovery. For fear that he might betray his own worries, Will spent many words on the weather, for a brilliant autumn was becoming a dismal early winter.

When John at last found a private moment with d'Artois and attempted to question him about the earl's designs on Blindley Heath, it was disastrous.

"He acted as if I'd gone off my head," said John that night to Will. "Are you sure you're not making up the whole thing?"

John was glaring at him. What could he say? *Was* he making it up? No.

"*No!* I heard what I heard."

John didn't seem convinced.

Two long weeks passed.

John was up and walking, his wound nearly healed and his cracked rib mending. He still was a difficult patient, but spent less time complaining; sometimes he even helped entertain the children.

One morning three weeks after the accident, Lady Elaine came into the nursery.

"John," she said, "Barber says you are well enough to return to the barracks."

John looked as though he might jump out of his skin.

"Today, milady?"

"Yes. However, you must wear this corset to protect your rib. Put it on over your shirt and it will keep you from harm in the course of your duties."

The corset was the lightest, most supple weave of leather and mail Will had ever seen.

"Anything, milady," said John.

"Will, you are to see to it that John has this on and properly fastened at all times."

She looked at him intently, her blue eyes so serious they were nearly black.

"Yes, milady," said Will. "I will be sure he wears it."

That morning as they crossed the bailey, Will slowed his pace and looked around before speaking softly.

"This confirms it," he said, poking John's side.

"What!"

"No one has ever worn a mail corset for a broken rib," said Will. "This is part of Lady Elaine's plan to protect you from other accidents."

John walked on a few steps before speaking.

"What about you?" he said. "What's to protect you?"

Will shrugged.

"When we are in the barracks or yard," said John, "I think it's best if I ignore you. But if ever you have need of me, signal like this." John signed a cross over his heart.

Will nodded and smiled. It was good to have someone to count on at Oxford Castle.

Back in the barracks, Will was under Squat Wat's rule again.

"*Rabbit!*"

"Yes, sir."

"Latrines tomorrow by sunup, and when Alfred the butler is through with you after the dinner hour, report to the stables."

"Yes, sir."

A new page appeared next to Will in the lineup in the yard. He was nearly as tall as Hubert and looked too old to be starting training. Squire Wat called him Turtle, which seemed to make him wince. When he could, Will would ask his real name.

D'Artois paired them for the broad sword, which was nearly as ridiculous as being paired with Hubert, though Squat Wat was certainly enjoying it.

"That's right, Rabbit, smack that slow old Turtle!"

Will lifted his sword off the ground and managed to make contact with Turtle. It was a light blow, just grazing his back. But suddenly, Turtle had tumbled over, landing, sprawled out, at Will's feet.

"Ha! Well, I'll be! The Rabbit *is* a match for the Turtle!"

Will was puzzled. There was no way that his blow had knocked the Turtle down.

"Get up, GET UP!" said Squire Wat. "Time for more punishment."

Turtle got slowly to his feet. He glanced briefly at Will. And though it seemed odd, Will could have sworn that Turtle winked at him.

X.
Wallingford

Turtle rarely spoke, telling Will only that his real name was Torrence, and that he came from the West Country near Wales. Once Will caught him juggling five bright-colored balls, which he quickly put away. Turtle could tumble off a horse and be back on again almost faster than Will's eyes could see him do it. Then he'd look at Will as if they were sharing a joke. But Will wasn't sure what that joke might be.

No matter what Will did or where he went, Turtle was there. Maybe he was one or two paces behind him, maybe out of sight, but *always* there. Will thought he'd rather wear John's corset than have Turtle always stepping on his shadow.

"No, you wouldn't!" said John. "I can hardly move, or breathe!"

"Well, you're stuck with it," said Will. "As I am stuck with Turtle."

And Squat Wat, *and* d'Artois, and cleaning piss pots,

mucking out the stables, and taking Latin lessons at night with Gervase the clerk.

It was many weeks before Will could keep his promise to Simon and go to Wallingford. Finally, one afternoon in mid-December, Will was free of duties and punishments. Squat Wat had Turtle busy scouring the knights' mail with sand to rid it of rust when Will stole to the stables. He saddled his mare as quickly and quietly as possible and set off.

As soon as Will had left the shadow of Oxford Castle, he was free! For the first time in weeks he felt safe from plots and intrigues. He was free from Turtle, Squire Wat, and d'Artois. The twelve miles to Wallingford were not long enough. He could have ridden forever.

Sunlight warmed the winter fields, bare now but for patches of stubble and snow. Will was warmed by the good woolen cloak that Lady Elaine had given him on Michaelmas. The cloak was in the earl's colors of silver gray and blue, and that guaranteed him safe passage through Oxfordshire. He carried Simon's parchment map in his sleeve and, as always, the wooden cross tucked inside his girdle.

The road was frozen hard, offering good footing for his mare. She, too, seemed glad to be out on the open road. Her exercise at Oxford had been limited to errands run from one field to the next. She tossed her head and snorted, sending out little clouds of vapor in the chill air. Soon they reached the Thames crossing. Will called to the bridge keeper, trying to sound as haughty as all in the earl's service.

"Make way," he said. "I go on business for my lord, Aubrey de Vere, earl of Oxford!"

"No need to shout. I ain't deaf," said the bridge keeper. He squinted up at Will through rheumy eyes. "I can see you're the earl's man. Go on then, serve your lord as I do mine."

The earl's man! Will sat higher in his saddle. Even if the villein was half blind, he'd called Will the earl's *man*.

Before long he was crossing the fields that bordered Simon's father's demesne. The gatekeeper let Will into the inner bailey, summoning a boy to take word of his arrival to Simon's mother, Lady Margaret.

Will was led through the great hall and up a small staircase to the solar. The manor of Wallingford was very much like Blindley Heath in size and furnishings. Though it was all new to him, it felt like home.

Lady Margaret put down her spinning and rose to greet him.

"Welcome, William Belet."

She had Simon's dark eyes and dimpled smile. Lady Margaret introduced Will to the other ladies in attendance and to Simon's sister, Edith. They all had black, sparkling eyes, dimples, and cheeks of dusky rose.

"Your eyes do not mistake you, Master Will," said Lady Margaret. "We are as alike as peas in a pod."

All the dark-eyed ladies laughed, all except Edith.

Lady Margaret sent to the kitchen for ale and cheese. They sat Will on the clothes chest and all the ladies perched on the bed, facing him. Lady Margaret made polite inquiries about Will and Oxford Castle.

"Now tell us about Simon," Edith broke in. "His letters from Godstone don't sound true. Do you think they can really make a monk out of my brother?"

"Edith!" said Lady Margaret. "Do you think *we* will ever make a *lady* out of you?"

Edith's dark curls were in a wild tangle and her tunic was none too clean. Edith scowled and Will bit his lip to keep from grinning.

"Simon gets on fine in the monastery," said Will, "in spite of all the rules."

"You mean he doesn't obey them," said Edith. "Just as I thought. They'll be packing him back to us before Christmas. Lent at the latest."

"I don't think the monks give up so easily," said Lady Margaret.

"He may want to stay," said Will. "Simon has a gift." He pulled out the map and handed it to Lady Margaret.

"My little rogue sat still to draw this?" she asked.

Edith peered over her shoulder as did the other ladies.

" 'Tis a wonder!" said Edith. "Look, Mother, he's even got old Tom's spotted sheep dog, and that must be Simon himself swimming in the fishpond."

For all the times Will had studied the map, he'd never noticed that.

"Please keep it," said Will.

"Thank you kindly," said Lady Margaret, and she pressed Will's hand.

"Mother, may I take Master Will skating? The fishpond has been frozen solid for nearly a week."

"You may," said Lady Margaret. "If Master Will wishes it."

"Skating?" said Will.

"I've been saving shinbones," said Edith. "Smith sharpened them for me and fitted them with leather straps and . . . You've never ice skated, have you?"

"No," said Will.

"I'm sure it will please you," said Edith, grinning at Will, her black eyes flashing.

He couldn't help but smile back, no matter what foolishness she had in mind.

A gray-haired knight entered the solar, pulling off his gauntlets and casting aside his cloak. He went directly to Lady Margaret and kissed her cheek.

"What's this?" he said. "A guest, and no ale — no victuals!"

"This is Master William Belet," said Lady Margaret, "page to Sir Aubrey de Vere."

"Yes, yes, the earl's page."

"My husband, Sir Brian Fitz Count," said Lady Margaret.

Will bowed.

"Sir John's second son?" asked Sir Brian.

"Yes, sir."

"Well, at last you've come! Welcome! Welcome!" He embraced Will, then looked around again. "Where's the drink? Where are the victuals?"

"Coming, my lord," said Lady Margaret.

"But we are going skating," said Edith.

"You'd send my dearest friend's son out into the cold without so much as a drop of ale to warm him?" asked Sir Brian.

"Very well," said Edith. "Ale."

"And victuals!" said Sir Brian.

"And then he's mine," said Edith.

"You two!" said Lady Margaret. "What will William Belet think?"

They all looked to Will. What should he say? He'd never met anyone quite like the Fitz Counts.

Finally Edith broke the silence.

"He thinks we're fopdoodles!" she said.

And they all laughed. Then the ale arrived with fine white bread, hard yellow cheese, and spiced pears.

"So tell me, Master Will," said Sir Brian. "What shall Aubrey de Vere do about the earl of Chester?"

"Begging your pardon, sir," said Will. "I don't understand the question."

"The earl of Chester, once the king's man, has

turned away from Stephen of Blois. Right now he holds his castle at Lincoln against Stephen and the king besieges him." Sir Brian drained his cup and Edith refilled it.

"Will Earl Aubrey go to help Chester?"

"I don't know," said Will.

"Don't know!" said Sir Brian. "Pages are supposed to know their master's business. This is important, lad. Chester is a wily dog and not entirely to be trusted. But his support could make the difference for England. If he fights for the rightful succession, Matilda could secure the crown for her son, Lord Henry, by Eastertide."

"I can find out, sir," said Will.

"Indeed you can," said Sir Brian. "Keep your eyes and ears open. England depends on the likes of Chester. If he will support Matilda, then there is still hope. Bring me news when you can. If the earl rides to Lincoln, then so do I."

Will was encouraged to eat and drink his fill. But before he was able to question Sir Brian more about Lincoln, Edith had dragged him off to the fishpond. Two servants followed them, carrying warmed stones and woolen blankets.

Edith taught Will how to fasten the shinbones to his boots with leather strips threaded through holes bored in the bones. She helped him up and, skating backward, pulled him forward onto the pond. The minute she let go of his hands, his feet slid out in opposite directions and Will went crashing down.

"That won't do!" said Edith laughing.

She helped him up and pulled him around as before.

"Now lean forward a little and bend your knees," she said. "Yes. That's it. Good. Very good."

"Yes, I think I've got it," said Will. Edith let go and Will lurched, skidded, and landed flat on his back.

Edith was laughing so hard she lost her balance and down she went.

"You're not very good," she said. "But don't worry. No one is his first time out."

Will didn't mind her merriment. It was so different from the scornful laughter of the pages of Oxford Castle. And Edith laughed loudest when *she* fell down.

Eventually Will could keep his legs under him for a complete turn around the pond. Edith was trying fancy spins, which more often than not sent her sprawling. After a while, she took Will by the hands and they skated together, Edith gliding backward, steadying Will.

"Does it suit you, Master Will?" she asked.

"Yes, I like the skating," said Will.

"And Oxford Castle, and training for knighthood?"

"I want someday to be as fine a knight as those who served Charlemagne. But it seems such a long way off," said Will. "I wish that I could wake up tomor-

105

row, already grown, already knighted and earning my honor."

"Yes, isn't the waiting for things terrible?" said Edith. "I'm nearly twelve, and still my life isn't settled upon."

"What would you have happen by morning?" asked Will.

"I don't know," said Edith. "I'd wake up with my own husband, manor, and children. Or perhaps I'd be the abbess at Fontevrault. What I really wish is to wake up a knight on my way to fight the infidels in Jerusalem."

Even a hoyden such as Edith could never be a knight.

"Someday," said Will, "you could make a pilgrimage to the Holy City."

"What a good idea, Will," said Edith. "In truth, the fighting doesn't interest me. But, oh, I want to go beyond Wallingford."

Even the humiliations and worries of Oxford Castle were better than sitting around waiting for life to begin. Will looked up and saw that the sun was hanging low in the western sky.

"God help me," he said. " 'Tis getting on evening. I must get back to Oxford."

"You should come warm yourself before starting out," said Edith. "You'll take a chill."

"I'll be all right," said Will. "As long as Squire Wat doesn't catch me coming in late."

"And you will come back?" asked Edith.

"I'll be back," said Will. "I give you my word."

Edith smiled.

"Tell Sir Brian when next I come, I'll bring him answers to his questions. And please excuse me to your lady mother, and thank her for her hospitality."

"Yes, yes, I will," said Edith. "But come soon. Father's favorite bitch is about to whelp. You can help me name the puppies."

Will rode his little mare hard. As he raced the darkening sky, he thought about what Sir Brian had said. No matter what the intrigues of Oxford Castle, a page *should* know his master's business. If Earl Aubrey helped the earl of Chester break the siege at Lincoln, it would give Empress Matilda and Lord Henry a powerful ally. With Chester's aid, King Stephen could be deposed and England would be safe. That was what mattered most to Will's father and Earl Aubrey. Will was always so busy trying to figure out Turtle and d'Artois, and to keep out of Squat Wat's way, he'd not been paying enough attention to the important things of the world. He had spent the past years longing to be out in the world. Well, here he was, out in the world, and acting like a scared little rabbit. It was time to move out of his safe burrow.

Will heard the bells for vespers as he rode over the Thames bridge. By the time he got to the castle and settled his mare in her stall, the service would surely be over. Squat Wat would catch him missing chapel and there would be hell to pay. Somehow Will would have to keep the punishment from interfering with his pledge to return to Wallingford. And Turtle would be ever more vigilant. It would be harder to elude him again. But he must.

XI.
The Earl's Will

At first Will thought his absence at vespers had gone unnoticed. Squire Wat cuffed him on the ear in passing, but that wasn't out of the ordinary. Perhaps St. Christopher had granted him protection. Will said a silent thankful prayer.

That night Will waylaid John outside the barracks when no one else was about. John pulled him into the dark stables and led him to a corner stall. The horses whinnied softly, their breath steaming the hay-sweet air.

"Will Earl Aubrey go to Lincoln Castle to aid the earl of Chester?" whispered Will.

"There is much talk about it," said John. "But I don't know. Why?"

"It will matter to us if he goes, won't it?"

"He wouldn't take us, if that's what you mean," said John. "Not with my injury and you . . . only just begun your training."

109

"It would matter to Blindley Heath?"

"Aye," said John. "Do you now look beyond the tip of your nose, brother? Yes. Chester could tip the balance for the empress and that affects us all."

Someone entered the stable, and John's hand closed on Will's arm, keeping him still. It was the first time John had touched him since his arrival in Oxford. It was very like Sir John's firm grip, filled with power and love.

Whoever had come to the stable finished his business and left quickly.

"Now that you have a question you will find an answer," said John. "Pay some attention to the earl whilst you serve his lady at the dinner hour."

They left the stable separately, John sending Will out first so he'd not be late to his bed.

Later Will lay in bed listening to the heavy breathing of the other pages. Only the Turtle slept silently, if indeed he slept. It hadn't occurred to Will that he and John might go to Lincoln Castle with Earl Aubrey. But once John said they wouldn't go, it started him thinking: why not? This could be his first real chance at battle. Even if he wasn't very good at the broad sword or quintain, he was skilled enough with the bow. Besides, pages went to battle to cook, nurse, and run errands. Only the knights and squires bore arms. But many things could happen in battle. Will might find a way to gain some small share of glory. It might bring his day of knighthood closer. Arthur was only fifteen when he became king of the Britons. He must have seen his share of combat before that. Perhaps there *was* a way for John and Will to go to Lincoln.

The next morning Lady Elaine summoned him to her chambers.

"Master Will Belet," she began, her voice harsh and her eyes flashing. "How dare you leave Oxford Castle without permission!"

"I beg your pardon," said Will, kneeling, "for having offended you."

"I wasn't offended," said Lady Elaine. "I was sore alarmed. And so was Torrence."

It would have been better had Squire Wat caught him. He'd rather have a beating in the stables than lose the good will of Lady Elaine.

"From now on you go nowhere without my leave and the company of Torrence of Cornwall."

Will bowed his head. There was no arguing with his lady. He'd not be able to see Edith again, after all.

"Now tell me where you went," she said, her voice gentling.

"I went to Wallingford," said Will. "To fulfill a pledge to Simon Fitz Count."

"No doubt you found a welcoming hearth there," said Lady Elaine. "Sir Brian and Lady Margaret would be very glad to see John Belet's son."

"Yes," said Will. "They were most kind."

"Very well," said Lady Elaine. "You may continue your acquaintance with Wallingford. Your father would be pleased for you to have Sir Brian as an ally."

"Thank you, milady," said Will. "*You* are most kind."

"Will, your father has placed great trust in me. I need your help not to betray that trust."

Will nodded. He'd do whatever she required for her sake and his father's. Even if it meant being yoked to Turtle.

"Milady, who is Torrence?"

"A lad from Cornwall," said Lady Elaine. "That is all you need to know."

Her voice was firm. The subject was closed. Will tried another approach.

"Does Earl Aubrey go to Lincoln to aid the earl of Chester?"

"Yes, I believe he will, after the Christmas feasts."

"Might I go too?" asked Will.

"Of course not," she said. "My lord cannot take an untried page into battle. At least on that account I can rest easy."

But Will could not. If he had to stay at Oxford, he'd remain the Rabbit forever. But perhaps Lady Elaine was wrong. Not even she could know for sure the earl's will.

The next few weeks raced by. The castle was in a

tempest preparing for the Christmas festivities. In addition to their regular duties, the pages were set to work helping the servants. All the lords who held land of Earl Aubrey would be coming to pay homage and renew their vows of fealty. With them would come their ladies, knights, and retainers. Oxford Castle had to be readied to shelter and entertain them all.

Will helped replace the floor rushes with new sweet-smelling hay. Then he and the other pages were sent to the forest for pine boughs and holly. The ladies wove them into garlands that the pages hung round the great hall and through all the apartments. Soon every corner of the castle smelled as fresh and pure as the king's forest. It was nearly as cold as the forest, too, in spite of fires blazing in every grate. The great hall was warm only where the earl sat, by the hearth. Mayhap grandeur and heat could not exist together. The hall at Blindley Heath was large enough to welcome all, but small enough that the least villein was warmed by the hearth. There was no doubt that Earl Aubrey cared little for comfort and much for show. The more Will studied his uncle, the more he saw that the earl concerned himself greatly with the outward signs of his power and prestige. But the welfare of those who served him, and especially the villeins who toiled for Oxford, didn't matter to him at all.

In preparation for the feasting, each ewer, bowl,

charger, and cup had to be polished with salt and vinegar until it shone like glass. Giselle the cook was in a constant rage. Will learned to duck before she could strike him.

The week before Christmas, Lady Elaine sent Will and Turtle to Wallingford with a letter for Lady Margaret. Will told Sir Brian what he'd learned of the earl's plans. Except for what Lady Elaine had told him it wasn't much. Will could study the earl's character but not discern his intentions. His uncle hardly spoke at dinner in the great hall. And his knights kept their own counsel as well.

Edith soon hurried them away to skate on the frozen pond. She dragged Will onto the ice, but Turtle didn't need any assistance. He was brilliant at it, skating rings around both Will and Edith.

Will still knew next to nothing about Turtle, even though he stayed as close to Will as a second skin. What he did know was that Turtle was the most ill-fitting name possible for him. Yet, when Turtle was near Squire Wat, the marshal, or the earl, he seemed to become duller and denser, his face going as cold and dumb as a reptile except for the quicksilver in his eyes.

Edith liked him well enough.

"Where did you learn to skate, Master Torrence?" she asked.

"London," said Turtle.

"You're so good."

Turtle nodded.

"Can you teach me the fancy turns?" she asked.

Turtle shrugged.

When it was nearing time to leave, Edith gave them each a pair of shinbones fitted with leather thongs.

"You could skate part way to Wallingford from Oxford Castle," she said. "Just follow the Thames and cross the fields. I'll show you a breach in the hedge that leads to a secret door in the back of the stables."

"We're so busy getting ready for the Christmas feasts," said Will. "I don't think Lady Elaine will send us back here until after the new year."

"But I shall see you before then!" said Edith. Her eyes were bright and her cheeks flushed.

"What do you mean?" asked Will.

"Mother and I are going with Father to the Oxford Feast! Is it true that three troupes of jugglers are coming from London?"

"And twenty pipers, a dancing bear, *and* a magician from the East!" said Will.

Turtle snorted.

"It's all true!" said Will. "And they say the magus can change his shape and tell the future."

Turtle rolled his eyes. But Edith seemed not to notice.

"I fear we shall be seated quite below the salt," she said. "Far from the choicest morsels and the jongleur's tales."

"Perhaps Lady Elaine can make sure your seat at

table isn't too far down," said Will. "*She* values your family greatly."

Edith squeezed Will's hand, and he felt a pleasant tingle.

"And will you still speak to your country friend once I'm inside the walls of the great castle?"

Will laughed. Edith didn't know for how little he counted at Oxford Castle.

"Perhaps Lady Elaine can spare me so that I may serve your family," he said.

Edith's eyes glittered, and her wild curls danced. She squeezed his hand again.

"Master Will," said Turtle. "We mustn't be late returning."

On the ride back to Oxford Will thought about Edith's dark eyes and the warm impression of her hand. Perhaps at the Christmas feasts he'd have a chance to hold her hand again. When they got back to the castle, Turtle stabled the horses while Will ran to Lady Elaine's apartments to deliver Lady Margaret's reply.

Dame Catherine pulled him up short as he was racing into the room. Will took off his cap. The earl and d'Artois were with Lady Elaine. No one seemed to notice Will. Lady Elaine and the earl were locked in an icy battle. Dame Catherine motioned for Will to rise and pulled him close.

"You cannot drag a new boy and an invalid into this campaign," said Lady Elaine.

"I can do whatever I wish," said the earl.

He and John were to go to Lincoln after all! It was the earl's will that they should go and Lady Elaine's that they stay. This was Will's chance to be part of a real battle — mayhap to prove himself. And just this once he sided with Earl Aubrey.

Lady Elaine and her lord spoke quietly, but their fury was clear from their stiff backs and their rancorous looks.

"My lord —" began Lady Elaine.

"Yes," said the earl. "*Your* lord. And I will not have you meddling further in my affairs."

Lady Elaine's face was dead white with two bright red patches on her cheeks.

"It will not do to threaten me," she said. "I am not alone and friendless in Oxfordshire. I am not like your first lady wife."

"Don't be so sure of your friends," said the earl. "If it suits, I'll have you walled up in a convent soon enough."

With that he left the room.

D'Artois moved closer to Lady Elaine, signaling her to be quiet. They all stood quite still, listening to the earl's retreating footsteps.

"Milady," said d'Artois, "do not put yourself at risk over this. I will protect them. Torrence will come too."

"I will not provoke a breach with the earl at *this* time," said Lady Elaine. "Indeed, I might find myself as powerless at Oxford as my husband's first wife."

Lady Elaine was still as white as ice and her hands were shaking. She glanced toward the door and for the first time noticed Will.

He went to her and, bowing low, handed her Lady Margaret's parchment scroll.

"So, Master Will," she said. "You will go with your lord to a glorious battle."

"I will fight for you, milady," said Will.

"No!" said Lady Elaine. "You will go to Lincoln, but you will not fight. You are not yet a warrior. Your duty is to return alive from Lincoln, that and that alone!"

Will nodded. He was hers to command. And yet if there came an opportunity to gain some measure of honor at Lincoln, he would disobey her to have his chance.

XII.
To Lincoln!

During the twelve days of Christmas feasting, knights on white chargers rode into the great hall carrying trays of the most astonishing food Will had ever seen. Peacocks had been plucked and roasted, then redressed in feathers, their beaks and feet painted gold. Giselle had contrived fantastical cockentrices, sewing a pig's head and shoulders to the hind of a capon, and the chicken's front to the back half of the pig.

But the lords talked of little else save the situation in Lincoln. The question most debated was whether Earl Aubrey would go to aid Chester. Will listened eagerly, wondering if he could trust what he heard and saw. Perhaps the earl had changed his mind. No one was sure what he'd do.

"They say the empress's half-brother Robert of Gloucester will ride to Lincoln."

"He should have no part in it. Chester is a dangerous friend. See how he treats the king, to whom he swore an oath!"

119

"I say a winter campaign is ill-omened."

"If Robert of Gloucester will aid Chester then all who support the empress should do the same!"

"Nay, it is Chester's battle."

"It might well be ours. All rests with Earl Aubrey."

"The young Lord Henry should come back from the Continent. It is time he was at his mother's side."

"Aye, his hour is coming soon, best he be in England."

What if Lincoln should be the battle to turn the tide for the empress and Lord Henry? Will had a hard time remembering his duties between the amazements of the feasts and the talk of the lords.

D'Artois and John were given the honor of serving Lady Elaine at the high table, so Will was able to help serve the Fitz Counts. Lady Elaine had made sure they were well placed at table and Will brought them all the best dishes. A special cook came from London to make marzipan and sugar sculptures. One was an exact replica of Oxford Castle, painted in bright colors and highlighted with real silver and gold.

Will was kept running from cock's crow to evensong. At night he fell on his cot — too tired to undress properly, too tired to dream. And he didn't mind at all. He was caught up in the great show for all the gentry of the earl's demesne. The only problem was that there was very little chance to be with Edith. He sought her out in the evenings when the trestle tables were cleared away and the company danced to the pipers from London.

"You've got a new tunic," said Edith.

"And new hose," said Will. "They even fit me. Is that a new gown?"

Edith twirled around, sending her crimson skirts billowing out like a flower. Her hair was tucked up in a snow-white linen wimple and her silk dress was very fine.

"Do you like it?" she asked.

Will nodded. He couldn't think of any words. Edith had become so much a lady. It was a great deal easier to talk to her when she looked a hoyden.

The grandest feast of all was prepared for Twelfth Night. Before the last course, an enormous pie was carried in by twenty knights all dressed in green brocade. The earl's steward marched in front, bearing a golden sword. Earl Aubrey raised his hand, and all in the great hall were silenced. The steward lifted high the sword, and when Earl Aubrey dropped his hand, the sword split open the pie.

Out leapt six acrobats, juggling golden apples studded with pearls! Everyone gasped, then burst into applause. Surviving that terrible golden blade was even more marvelous than the juggling.

After the last course the tables were pushed back and the benches arranged so that all faced Earl Aubrey. One by one, lords of the land came and knelt

121

before him. Each man's hands were clasped together in supplication as he put his hands within Earl Aubrey's, placing himself and his family under the lord's protection. In return for the land each held of the earl, he swore his support in war and peace. It was very solemn. There was no music in the hall and no talking.

The earl bid each lord rise, then bestowed upon him a magnificent gift. Sumptuous robes were given, precious jewels, and arms encrusted with gems. The gift-giving was as solemn as the oath.

In his turn Sir Brian swore his allegiance for the holding of Wallingford and received a sword of the finest steel, its scabbard and hilt patterned over with gold inlay and mother-of-pearl.

"Thank you, my liege," said Sir Brian. His voice rang out as proudly he bore away his gift, carrying it on high for all to see.

But none looked so proud as the earl. Only the noblest lord could give such gifts. His largesse ranked him with kings! His robe of midnight velvet lined with vair was the finest in the hall. His face, cold and stern as always, seemed the correct face for his role. He looked the most noble lord of the land. And the hundreds of lords gathered were putting their lives in his hands. If only Will could believe that his uncle was, indeed, the worthiest, most noble lord in England.

Lady Elaine, dressed in emerald velvet and vair, sat

under the azure baldaquin at his side. Will was sure she would have outshone even Queen Guinevere. And not for a moment did her face or manner betray any discord between her and Earl Aubrey. Her fate, even more than that of the gathered lords, rested in the great earl's hands.

"That man is capable of anything!" Dame Catherine had said when Will had asked if the earl would harm Lady Elaine. "He'll seal her up in a convent, quick as you please, if it suits him," she said. "Just as he did his first lady wife."

And then what could Will do to help her?

The last of the noble lords had given his vow, received his gift, and returned to the side of the hall. The earl remained standing, silent a moment. Then he spoke, his deep voice carrying throughout the hall.

"The most valorous earl of Chester holds his castle in Lincoln against King Stephen. This is our moment to win Chester to the side of Empress Matilda for the rightful succession of Lord Henry. Earl Robert rides to fight for Chester. And I say we ride with him. What say you?"

With one voice all the men shouted:

"TO LINCOLN!"

And again they shouted and again, until the very stones of the castle trembled.

"TO LINCOLN! TO LINCOLN! TO LIN-COLN!"

Will shouted with all his might, his voice part of the glorious roar. Lincoln would be his battle, too.

Earl Aubrey and Earl Robert would break the king's siege of Lincoln and win the earl of Chester over to the rightful cause of the empress. Will would be there. Lincoln would be his battle, too.

"Hurrah!" he shouted. "HURRAH!"

Sir Brian Fitz Count clapped him on the back.

"That's the spirit, lad! That's the spirit!"

Will grinned. Then he caught d'Artois's grim look, and all the hot excitement drained out of him.

XIII.
A Winter Campaign

They only had a fortnight to prepare in order to meet up with Earl Robert's forces and march on Lincoln. Everyone in the castle worked furiously to ready the vast army and all its supplies. Will polished arms and mail with sand until his bones ached and his hands were raw. When Squat Wat was satisfied that all was gleaming and mirror bright, Will was sent to the constable to help pack the supply train. There were no lessons, no meals. Will ate on the run and often slept where he stood. The castle was marching to the drumbeat of battle and *nearly* all kept in step. In out-of-the-way corners of the keep, Will heard men complain.

"Never mind the foul weather," said one. "It is folly to march over frozen fields with no grazing for the horses and even less to eat for the men."

"The peasants always have well-stocked larders, though they may be hidden," another replied.

"That's right, starve the peasants. Then who will do the planting come spring?"

"That's not your worry."

The cotters at Blindley Heath had just enough put by to last them through the spring planting, and that was in a good year. Sir John often distributed manor stores to see them through. They could ill afford to feed a hungry levy. But perhaps that wasn't Will's worry, either.

The one who most seemed to enjoy the preparations for battle was Squat Wat.

"To the stables! To the smith! Hone this dagger! Hop Rabbit, HOP!"

Will did hop. He did everything he was told. And he listened carefully to all that was said of the coming march and battle. He would know as much as he could. He'd not be surprised and frightened as he was in the king's forest. He'd be ready for the blood of battle. He'd stand firm. He'd do something exceedingly valiant. But what?

John was a worry. The Christmas revels, and all the extra work since then, had him looking pale, with purple rings hollowing his eyes. He never complained, but his wound must still pain him. D'Artois limped and clumped as before, though now he was fired up with new energy. And when Will was sent running to the far corners of the castle, he'd often find d'Artois briskly attending to his own business. The only one untouched by the furious preparations was the Turtle. He seemed to move as if under water. Each action was so slow and deliberate it drove the squire mad.

"Bless it, Turtle, I said spit and polish on the double!"

"Yes, sir!" said Turtle, and he bent once more to polishing the harnesses as slowly as before, with just a wrinkle of laughter about his eyes.

There was no chance to ride to Wallingford before they set out, no way to say a proper farewell to Edith. There'd been an awkward parting after the Twelfth Night feast. If her hair had hung in tangled curls, and her cheeks had been flushed from skating, then Will would have been able to tell her of his plans and worries. But Edith coiffed in fine linen and dressed in silk had made him too nervous.

"Bye," he mumbled.

"Take care," she said. "I'll be waiting for you."

"Well, good-bye."

He wanted to give her something or have something of hers to take with him. She leaned close to him and kissed him lightly on the cheek, like the brush of moth wings.

"God be with you, Master Will."

On the eve of their departure for Lincoln, Lady Elaine sent for Will. Dame Catherine brought him a steaming bowl of porridge and cream glazed with honey.

"Sit and eat while you listen," said Lady Elaine. "And listen well."

She sat across from Will, her eyes darkened with gravity.

"You must watch out for each other. Torrence has orders *never* to leave your side. The chaos of battle can provide ample cover for misdeeds. Stay alert. Keep watch of John's back as well as your own. Obey instantly anything Sir Ranulf d'Artois asks of you. Obey him as you would your father. Do you understand?"

Will swallowed a hot lump of porridge.

"Yes, milady."

Before she dismissed him, Lady Elaine gave him a shirt of mail as fine and supple as cloth, and a pouch with many pockets. On each pocket was embroidered a tiny flower, showing the healing herb within.

"Wear the shirt and keep the pouch tied to your girdle. I fear you will have need of both," she said, and took his hands in hers. "Come back safely, Master Will."

He would do that and more. Somehow he'd help further the cause of the empress and Lord Henry. He'd come back to Oxford with honor.

They left at daybreak in a driving, icy rain. It was a huge procession, headed by Earl Aubrey and two hundred knights and squires. The greatest lords rode closest to the earl. D'Artois, John, and the other young squires were somewhere toward the back. Sir Brian

Fitz Count rode nearer the middle. Astride his enormous charger, the earl could be seen from as far back as the baggage train, the plumes on his helmet waving briskly in the wind and rain. Will and Turtle and the other boys rode alongside the baggage. They were jokingly called the kitchen guard. Behind the knights and the baggage marched four hundred foot soldiers. Half were archers and well trained. The others carried axes, pikes, shields, and clubs; some of the poorest had only a scythe or mattock.

Heavy mantles lined with rich furs kept the lords dry and warm. The pages and most of the foot soldiers wore brown oilcloth capes over their woolen cloaks which kept out most of the rain, although fingers of icy water trickled down Will's neck and the sleet lashed at his face.

"Looks like the march of the Brown Friars," said Squire Wat, and he spat on the ground.

He was wrong. The Earl's levy was absolutely splendid. A great standard was borne before the earl in the colors of Oxford with the lion rampant at its center. The lion had been King Henry's device, and now was used by Empress Matilda and her son, Lord Henry. The vassals of the earl, like Sir Brian Fitz Count and his men, rode under their banners. The colors of red, green, and golden yellow on the shields and banners glowed with a strange brightness on the dark morning. The horns sang out, leading the army forward. It was more wonderful than the feast of Twelfth Night. That was mere diversion — this was war. And Will was in it!

Lady Elaine stood on the battlements with her attendants, watching the levy depart. And though she followed the earl with a steady gaze, he spared not a look for her. Dame Catherine waved to Will, and directed Lady Elaine's attention to the baggage train. Lady Elaine smiled at him, and that was his last view of her.

The march to Lincoln was a nightmare of winter rains and mud. Then Will heard many complaints about the folly of a winter campaign.

"In January a man should be by his hearth with a flagon of ale. Time enough for war in spring and summer."

The baggage train was often mired. Will spent much of the journey hauling stones to fill in the mud holes. In spite of the foul weather they traveled nearly fifteen miles a day.

Two days' ride from Lincoln they began to see the effects of King Stephen's army. He'd gone to Lincoln to punish the earl of Chester and had begun with the earl's peasants. Village after village had been plundered and then burned to the ground. Not one soul remained in sight.

"Is no one left?" asked Will.

"Likely many survive," said Turtle. "But they're hiding deep in the forests."

"But we've come to help them," said Will. "They should be glad to welcome us."

"Ha!" said Turtle, without any mirth. "Welcome the jackal once the wolf has passed by? We are taking their last morsels."

It was true. The scouts and foraging parties were rounding up the few stray animals and gleaning what was left of the winter wheat in the fields.

"The peasants will starve," said Will.

Turtle shrugged.

"That's what happens when the lords make war. The peasants die."

When King Arthur did battle, thought Will, it was against the enemies of England. He didn't wage war against peasants. Will's father shared the stores of Blindley Heath to help his peasants get through the winter.

Earl Aubrey's men certainly wouldn't die of starvation. They were well provided for on the march north. Stores were requisitioned from every manor and village. What of those villages and manors? Wasn't the earl's levy eating up the stores they'd carefully hoarded to see them through the winter? Yet that was God's design. The village priest had said so, and Will's father had explained it many times: "The clergy prayed for all, the knights fought for all, and the peasants worked for all. Each had his place in the divine plan." Will's rightful place was marching with the rest of the earl's men. All was as it was meant to be. And yet . . . Turtle was right. They *were* like jackals eating the peasants' last crumbs. And knights should be protecting the peasants, as did King Arthur, as did John Belet. It would take the true heir to the throne of England to set things right again.

Besides the food from the villages and manors, hunting parties were sent out each dawn with the scouts to bring back fresh meat. The peasants might hide in the forests, but they risked hanging if they hunted there.

John and d'Artois were often included in the hunting parties. Will saw less of John now than he had at Oxford Castle. It was hard to obey Lady Elaine's orders to watch out for his brother when he only caught glimpses of him in the evening by the fires.

When he could, when Squat Wat wasn't after him to fetch, clean, or carry, Will would sit close to John and the young squires and listen to their talk. As always, Turtle was by his side, though Turtle seemed to have little interest in the war talk.

"They say the king has a huge levy at Lincoln. And that the earl of Essex prepares now to bring him more men," said Percival.

"Essex has none to spare," said d'Artois. "His men are too busy sacking defenseless castles."

That drew a grim laugh. All had cause to worry about their homes whilst they marched north to Lincoln.

"After we rout the king's levy, I say we take on Essex. Let's make short work of all the scoundrels," said Reynard.

"Fine words indeed," said d'Artois. "If your deeds match up to them then we shall have a small chance of success at Lincoln."

"Gloom and doom!" said Manfred.

"Victory is easily spoken," said d'Artois. "And hard won. England is torn asunder while young hotheads talk of glory."

The young squires laughed at d'Artois, all except John.

"Sir Ranulf has fought on many fields," he said. "Give him his due."

John's deep voice stopped their taunts. It was very like when Will's father spoke to his men.

"Has any of us known battle? All we know are boys' games. When the games are deadly, will we be so cocksure?"

A silence fell. Like as not, some among them would not return from Lincoln. Will studied John. Something made him seem much older than the other squires. And d'Artois! Though only a few years older than John, he seemed a veritable graybeard. The nearness of death had changed them.

Suddenly the full weight of it struck Will — death was abiding at Lincoln.

XIV.
Battle

Midnight on the tenth day they came to the hamlet of Metheringham, or what was left of it, two hours' march from Lincoln Castle. There they met up with the levies of Robert of Gloucester and the earl of Bedford. Altogether they were a force of some fifteen hundred men. Will looked for a familiar banner or shield, but none of the knights of Surrey were marching to Lincoln. They made camp with only a few fires and had cold rations for supper, as the earl hoped to keep their numbers secret. Many campfires would have betrayed them to King Stephen's scouts.

The rain had finally ceased. The cold, clear night sparkled with stars and the glimmer of a crescent moon. Will hurried through his duties and sought out John. He caught the lilt of the young squires' laughter not far from where the horses were picketed. Will slipped in behind his brother, outside the ring of young men.

The earl had sent round extra rations of mead to warm the men in place of the missing fires. The flagon was passed to John just as Will was sitting down. John took a draught and passed it to Will.

"Here, brother," said John. "Warm yourself."

"Me?" said Will. Usually John ignored him when he sat with the squires.

"Have I another brother?"

Will took the flagon and drank deeply. A river of fire raced down his throat, into his belly, far stronger than any spirits served at Oxford Castle. Will sputtered and coughed.

"Drinks like a girl," said Reynard.

"Or a rabbit," said d'Artois. And they all laughed.

Will took another long draught, this time without coughing. And this made them laugh more.

Earl Aubrey, flanked by his marshal and Sir Godfrey of Bedford, approached them.

"I'm glad there is reason for mirth among my young fighters," he said, and instantly the laughter died.

"Tomorrow may end your apprenticeship. Serve well your knights and obey them lest your youth lead you to a foolish death."

The earl's cold gaze rested briefly on John as he said, "foolish death." John didn't flinch, but Will couldn't help but shudder.

"We do battle for Empress Matilda and Lord Henry, the rightful heir of England. If we succeed there will be great rewards. Fight with your hearts and souls and win your spurs tomorrow at Lincoln!"

"Hurrah!" they shouted. "For Matilda! For Henry! For England!"

The earl opened a new flagon, drank once, then passed it round again before leaving. And soon after d'Artois bade them sleep.

Will returned to the baggage train where he made ready his own pallet next to Turtle.

But he could not sleep.

John would be fighting with d'Artois under the standard of Bedford, on the far right flank. Will thought it odd that they wouldn't be with Earl Aubrey's men. But neither d'Artois nor John commented on it, so Will didn't either. His orders were to stay near the baggage train. How could he watch out for John or have any chance at glory back with the baggage? Once the fighting started he'd have to find his way to the front line.

Will fell into a restless sleep filled with dreams of the earl leering at him, brandishing his sword, and saying "foolish death" over and over until the words had no meaning at all.

Squire Wat kicked him awake.

"Up, Rabbit! Water the horses and fetch their feed!"

Will rose numbly in the frigid dawn. He shuffled toward the horses, his limbs cold and stiff. How could a day of glory begin so basely?

Once he'd tended the horses, Will helped himself to an oatcake and a dipper of ale from the cook tent and then went to find John.

The priests were saying Mass under the three baronial standards.

All of Earl Aubrey's knights, squires, some of the yeomen, and the earl himself had gathered round the Oxford priest on bended knee with heads bowed. Will found John and d'Artois and took his place beside them as the priest offered up a prayer for their safe-keeping.

> *Thou, O Lord, art just and powerful:*
>   *O defend our cause against the face*
> *of the enemy.*
>   *O Lord of hosts, fight for us, that*
> *we may glorify thee.*
>   *O Lord, arise, help us, and deliver*
> *us for thy Name's sake.*

When the priest finished, d'Artois and many of the others made the sign of the cross, and bending to the earth, took a small piece of soil in their mouths.

"What was that about?" asked John as they left to arm themselves.

Will wanted to know too — it was such a humble gesture for d'Artois — but *he* dared not ask.

"It meant," said d'Artois, "that I have accepted death and burial in the earth, which I may well find at Lincoln this day."

After that, John and Will were silent. Many men would die even if the battle went well. But if King Stephen held the day they would lose more than their hope for Matilda to be Lady of England. The king would not spare any who had ridden against him. Only the richest would be held for ransom. Many, many more would die ignobly, slaughtered as prisoners.

John helped d'Artois arm for the battle. Over a linen shirt d'Artois wore a quilted tunic to protect him from the chain mail of the hauberk. Over the hauberk, he wore a linen tabard emblazoned with the earl's device. Then John helped wrap d'Artois's legs with leather strips, and lastly, he fastened his spurs and helped him on with his helmet. In turn, Will helped John with his hauberk, hose, and helmet.

D'Artois carried a lance for the first charge, a sword for the combat that would follow, and a great kite-shaped shield. John had a long dagger, battle-ax tucked in his girdle, and smaller round shield.

Morning rations of mead were being handed out. Flagons passed from man to man. John was about to drink when d'Artois stopped him.

"That is fool's courage, Squire John. Today you will need your wits about you."

John looked hard at d'Artois.

"Aye," he said, and passed the flagon to Reynard. The other young men had drunk deeply and were beginning to swagger and boast.

"I shall slay a score of men and take the earl of Sheffield as my hostage," said one.

"And I shall take Norwich, for he is worth twice the earl of Sheffield," retorted another.

"MOUNT UP!"

"MOUNT UP!"

The order ran through the camp like fire.

"Keep safe, brother," said John.

"Aye," said Will. "And you."

John grimaced and lightly boxed Will's ear.

Will raced back to the baggage train before Squire Wat could flog him. He rescued his mare from the snarl of picket lines as the squires sought out the knights' horses and their own. Turtle was waiting there, mounted on his roan and holding Will's bow and arrows.

But after the scramble for the horses all was in order. The knights rode under the three standards of Bedford, Gloucester, and Oxford. On the flanks and between each block of knights marched a company of archers, backed by the infantry.

They marched at a steady pace, holding their formation. Clouds of vapor, smelling sweetly of mead, were tinged golden by the first rays of the sun. Horses whinnied and snorted, but the men had little to say.

Within an hour, the turrets of Lincoln Castle could be seen rising over the plain. As they drew near their lines widened out as more men rode to the front, readying themselves for the first charge. The baggage train, far to the back for the march from Oxford, moved up as they got closer to Lincoln. Will found himself only thirty yards or so from the standard bearers. Once the battle began, it wouldn't be difficult to get to the front with John and d'Artois.

Squire Wat would be joining the knights for the first charge. Now he shouted orders to the yeomen who would stand guard of the baggage during the battle.

"Keep a sharp eye that there's no looting," he said. "One missing piece of silver and I'll have your heads."

"And you," he said, turning to Will and Turtle. "Help disarm the prisoners and tend the wounded. The devil take you if you trip up the fighting men."

Robert of Gloucester called a halt when they reached bowshot of the king's levy, which commanded a slight rise of land to the left of Lincoln Castle and beside a greenwood. Will had a clear view of them, more men than he had dreamed possible. They stretched out, a line of bristling spears and lances, sunlight glinting on their helmets and shields. King Stephen was well prepared to hold his position at Lincoln Castle. Will's teeth chattered, and it wasn't the cold. How could they win against this?

There was a quiet time as archers and knights made ready. Many said a final prayer or had a last pull at the flagons of mead. Will fingered the cross tucked in his girdle — Simon's gift — and prayed for courage. He heard a faint cheer from Lincoln Castle that was soon blown away by a gust of wind.

Robert of Gloucester gave the signal, and the horns of war sang forth.

"War," they shrieked. "War! War! War!"

Then came a great, terrifying shout as both sides hurled themselves into battle.

The forces of Gloucester, Oxford, and Bedford lowered their lances and charged at full gallop into the oncoming knights of King Stephen. The archers let fly a volley of arrows aimed high over the heads of their own knights. The shafts traced a steep arc that came raining down on King Stephen's men. Meanwhile the king's archers loosed a storm of arrows on the earl's forces. There was the clatter of steel on steel and the screams of horses, wounded and toppling their riders. And then came the great clash as horses met in midfield. Many knights were unhorsed. Other mounts stumbled over them and threw their own riders.

Will was far enough away to perceive the whole of it and close enough to see the grim struggle as men fought and died. This was the fighting he'd witnessed in the king's forest magnified a thousand times over. And though he saw it with his own eyes, he could not believe anything could be so horrible.

Will sat on his mare, a frightened rabbit indeed. What in the name of heaven could he do in that horrid tangle of men? All his hopes of glory, of somehow making a difference in the battle, were but a boy's fancy, a rabbit's dream. He'd be lucky not to dishonor himself by fainting.

The fighting grew worse. Lances were cast aside as the knights drew their swords, fighting man to man. Blood stained the winter fields.

Nothing. Not a thing could he do out there. And yet, as frightened as he was, he had to go. More clearly than ever he understood John's danger. For in that melee who would notice murder? Already he'd hesitated too long.

Will urged his mare forward and sought out John. He edged his way to the side of the battlefield where flew the standard of Bedford.

"Idiot!" screamed Turtle. "Your orders were to stay put. You'll be getting us both killed."

"I have to find John," said Will.

Turtle gave him a grim look. "Can you at least keep out of the way of the archers?"

Will nodded. They skirted the right flank, and when they spotted d'Artois, they plunged into the worst of it.

Knights, covered from head to foot in metal and leather, hardly looked like men. Their faces and names were replaced by the bright-colored devices on their shield and tabards. They could have been machines of war, but the coursing blood from brow and limb gave the lie to that as did the man smells of sweat and excrement.

Men were fighting mostly on foot with swords, pikes, and axes. Already the ground was littered with the dead and wounded, both horses and men, and slippery with their blood and entrails. Knights fought, hemmed in, often tripping on their fallen comrades.

Will steadied himself and his mare — he'd be of little help to John in a swoon — and pushed on. As dangerous as it was, Will and Turtle moved with some impunity amongst the fighting men, for there was no honor to be had in killing mere boys.

"Master Will," called Turtle, his voice urgent above the clamor, and pointed to their left. Had he come too late?

D'Artois on horseback was matching swords with one of the king's knights. John, on the ground, was fending off the attack of four yeomen. But these were not King Stephen's men. Will was sure he'd seen at least one of the knaves in the earl of Bedford's camp. These were assassins!

"D'Artois!" shouted Will. "D'ARTOIS!"

Meanwhile he launched an arrow into the blackguard whose axe was poised over John's head.

D'Artois dealt a killing blow to the king's knight and turned his horse to face John's attackers. He hacked at them with his mighty blade and soon the ground around them was a sea of agony.

Will and Turtle inched in closer. John had a gash on his shield arm and his face was covered in blood. D'Artois was finishing off the last of the yeomen when one of King Stephen's knights bore down upon him. And the next thing Will knew, d'Artois was on the ground with the slain, his lifeblood draining away.

His killer soon fell into the blood-soaked mud, hit by Turtle's arrow.

Will leapt from his mare, knelt by d'Artois, and took off his helmet.

"Ah, Rabbit," said d'Artois with his last breath. And then he died.

"We must get John back to the baggage train," said Turtle, and he slid off his horse. John, who a moment before had been defending his life, had now sunk to the ground. "Help me!" yelled Turtle.

Will left d'Artois in the mud and helped load John's dead weight onto Turtle's roan.

They found a path through the horror and somehow made it back alive to the baggage train.

XV.
Hollow Victory

"You did what you could," said Turtle.

"I did nothing," said Will.

"You saved John."

"D'Artois saved John, and then he died."

"Every knight goes into battle knowing he may die," said Turtle.

"D'Artois was certain of it."

And Turtle couldn't argue with that.

"Your arrow killed one of John's attackers," he said. "Did you note that that yeoman looked familiar?"

"So you saw it, too," said Will.

Turtle nodded. "Assassins," he said. "It was as Lady Elaine feared. At least you didn't get us killed."

Will had dressed and bound John's wounds. The shield arm would heal. He was much more concerned about the head injury, for John was a long time coming to, and once awake he remained muddled.

But Will had little time to worry over John. The

battle raged on, and it was impossible to tell which side held the advantage. All Will knew were the needs of the fallen men. He worked with the barber surgeon from Oxford, doctoring the wounded. Only those that could be helped were brought back to the makeshift camp behind the baggage train. Those with severe head injuries or stomach wounds died, often where they'd fallen, and were buried beneath the hedgerows.

In the evening, at the close of the day's fighting, Turtle, Will, and a few strong yeomen were sent to the battleground to rescue those wounded who might recover. Wounded nobles, especially the enemy lords, who'd fetch a fat ransom were carried from the field in the midst of battle and treated immediately, lest they die before a ransom could be collected.

Will treated noble and yeomen alike, as best he knew how. Over a hundred times a day he blessed Lady Elaine for her gift. The barber had much skill, especially at setting broken bones, but he knew little of potions and had brought only a few herbs.

It was awful work, worse than anything Will could have ever imagined. He went to his bed at night, haunted by the cries of the wounded and the agonies of the dying. Lucky were those whose death came swiftly, those who were dead before they knew the terror of dying. Will saw some of the bravest and boldest reduced to mewling babes as their life blood drained away. How was it that the jongleurs could sing glorious tales of battle when it was really such a grim, miserable business?

The evening of the second day of fighting, Will and Turtle found Squire Wat crushed under a dead horse. He was alive, but only just. He'd been badly wounded even before the damage caused by the horse.

"Help me, Rabbit," he said. "Save me!"

He'd not survive the night, and there were others who needed Will's help more. But he couldn't leave Squat Wat to such a pitiful death, alone on the frozen ground.

"I'll do what I can," said Will, and he had three yeomen carry the squire back to camp.

Will made him a strong draught that numbed his pain and let him pass peacefully to . . . where? A knight who died fighting in a just cause was guaranteed a place in heaven. But Squire Wat was no knight, and Will hoped he'd have his share of time in purgatory scouring piss pots.

Baron Ickworth of Newmarket was captured by Earl Aubrey and brought to Will early in the third day's battle. He had a deep gash on his shoulder. Will attended to the wound and brewed a potion that eased the burning pain.

"Where did you learn your skill, lad?"

"From my good mother, Lady Alice of Blindley Heath, and Lady Elaine of Oxford Castle," said Will.

"They've taught you well," said the lord. "I'm grateful to have fallen into your hands."

Will bowed and went to help the barber sew the stump of a knight's amputated leg.

Sir Brian Fitz Count looked for Will each evening. So far he'd escaped the battle unscathed.

"I'm a tough old bird," he said. "And lucky, too."

"How goes the battle, sir?" asked Will.

"It's hard to say," said Sir Brian. "The king outnumbers us but I think we outfight him."

Sir Brian looked hard at Will. "You are looking sickly, lad, and that will not do. Eat your victuals and get some rest."

Will tried. But very little food would stay in his stomach. Meat, especially, made him gag.

"You should take your own medicine," said Turtle. "Haven't you an herb to calm your gullet?"

Will drank chamomile and mint infusions, but that couldn't cure what ailed him. Meanwhile the fighting and doctoring went on.

But on the fourth day of battle, February second, Candlemas Day, came a great stroke of good fortune: King Stephen was isolated from his knights and captured by Earl Robert of Gloucester and his men.

"They say," said Turtle, "that the king was betrayed by his own knights."

Taking Stephen of Blois prisoner meant an instant

victory. This was the miracle that might well save England from further strife. With King Stephen captive the throne was empty. It was the long-awaited victory, the main chance for Empress Matilda and Lord Henry. This was much more than had been hoped for when the armies set out to aid the earl of Chester.

The king was mounted on his charger. Unlike other noble prisoners his helmet was removed and his hands shackled. Surrounded by their knights, the earls of Bedford, Gloucester, and Oxford led him up to Lincoln Castle. The gates were thrown wide open and the besieged swarmed out onto the battlefield, chasing down what men of the king could be found. The bells of the chapel rang a Te Deum and shouts of triumph filled the air.

Will heard it all from afar. But the victory did not drown out the cries of the wounded in his care. Nor did the victory restore John's wits or bring back d'Artois. All that Will could have hoped for England had come to pass. The battle of Lincoln might well mean the end of strife in England. But for Will, the Lincoln battle would always be a reminder of what he hadn't done. D'Artois was dead. John was gravely injured. If only Will had acted sooner he might have *done* something. Now he must go back and face the sadness and disappointment of Lady Elaine. All his hopes were ashes in his mouth.

The day after Candlemas, a feast was held in the great hall of Lincoln Castle to celebrate the victory. The earl of Chester and his brother, William de Roumare, sat at the high table surrounded by the most noble earls of England, including the great barons held for ransom. Even though they were prisoners, the captured lords feasted with their enemies. Will and Turtle were called upon to help serve. The rare dainties and fancy dishes sickened Will even more than had the stench of battle. He held the platters as far from his nose as possible, and keeping his jaw clenched managed not to retch and disgrace himself further.

As Will offered a platter of gingered carp to Baron Ickworth and Earl Aubrey, who shared a trencher, the baron said, "This is a coming lad, Earl Aubrey. You must be glad of his service."

The earl regarded Will as coldly as ever, so his answer came as a complete surprise.

"Will Belet has always served me well," said the earl. "And he shall be amply rewarded on our return to Oxford."

The earl's face showed no sign of mirth. But was this some sort of jest, or threat? Turtle had to pinch Will to get him to bow and move on.

"What did he mean by that?" asked Will that night when no one else was near.

Turtle shrugged.

"You'll have to wait and see," he said. "The earl could be a mummer or a priest; he keeps well disguised the true cast of his mind."

That night, back at the camp, the image of the earl's stony gaze tormented Will as much as those scenes on the battlefield he couldn't forget.

Two days later, when the men and horses were well rested, they began the triumphal march back to Oxford. John, in spite of his protests, rode on a pallet in the wagon with the cook and smith. Will hoped the jolting ride wouldn't do him further harm. Earl Robert of Gloucester was bringing the king, in fetters, to Bristol, where he'd remain imprisoned. No ransom would be great enough to free the king. Now was Empress Matilda's chance to win the throne.

Earl Aubrey was returning to Oxford Castle a mightier lord than ever. He'd won a great victory.

"And the empress will be grateful," said Turtle. "When she is Lady of England and the succession guaranteed for Lord Henry, the earl will be well rewarded for his trouble."

"He fought to help her cause," said Will.

"Aye, and for a piece of King Stephen's vast holdings."

Turtle was smiling grimly. Was that the real reason Earl Aubrey had gone to Lincoln — not so much to help the empress as to increase his own estate?

The earl's men had all come away from the battle of

Lincoln richer than when they'd set out. They had the plunder from the field and soon would have the captured knights' ransoms. Even the humblest villein gained a new pair of boots, or perhaps a dead man's sword. The men bragged of their bounty and were proud to have been the earl's soldiers. Earl Aubrey had reason to be well satisfied . . . except that for every five men who marched out of Oxfordshire, only four returned.

And Will suspected that his uncle might regret that John Belet still lived.

The weather remained clear, though bitterly cold. All were weary, yet eager for their homes. So they pushed hard, covering nearly twenty miles a day. The closer they came to Oxford, the more Will dreaded seeing Lady Elaine. She'd had confidence in him, and it had come to this: John was half alive and d'Artois was buried in the churchyard of Lincoln. She wouldn't *say* anything. But Will dreaded the sorrow he'd find in her eyes.

As the earl's levy had swollen on their march north when bands of knights along the way had ridden out to join them, now the army shrank as the knights turned off the main road to return to their manors.

Half a day's journey from Oxford, Sir Brian rode back to the baggage train to bid farewell to Will.

"You're still too pale, lad," he said. "When the earl can spare you, come to Wallingford and we shall put roses on your cheeks."

Sir Brian embraced him, and Will nearly cried, the strong grasp was so like his father's. He wished that he were headed toward the welcoming warmth of Blindley Heath, although he was glad not to be the herald of d'Artois's death and John's new wound. Sir John and Lady Alice would be sorely grieved.

They rode through Oxford Town at twilight, and the streets rang out with the cheers of the townfolk. Women leaned from the upper-story windows, their wimples painted softly gold with candle glow. Boys danced alongside the knights, following them all the way to the gates of Oxford Castle.

The villeins poured out of their cottages, some carrying their half-eaten supper, to cheer their lord's return. Not all cheered. There were the wails of wives and mothers whose husbands and sons would not return.

The courtyard of Oxford Castle was packed when, at last, Will's mare rode through the gatehouse. Servants ran to help the warriors. Giselle the cook was waving her iron ladle and shouting "Hurrah!"

But for all the cheering and bustle, something was terribly wrong. Will looked across the courtyard to where he'd first seen the beautiful Lady Elaine as she'd welcomed home her lord. Her place was empty!

Perhaps she'd gone closer to greet the earl and was obscured by the tall knights. Will stood in his stirrups and craned his neck. No. She wasn't there. Neither were any of her ladies.

The earl seemed not to notice her absence. Had he sent her away? Was she imprisoned? Was she alive? Will turned to Turtle.

"Say nothing," said Turtle. "And show nothing. I will tell you later."

Later! How could he wait for later? He was about to say "Tell me now!" when he caught the earl's eye. He was watching Will. And his eyes held a question.

Will dug his nails into his palms and did his best to smooth the worry and fear from his face.

XVI.
Gone

"Where is she?" asked Will.

"Shhh!" Turtle hushed him, then slipped sound-lessly along the length of the battlement. He must have been checking to make sure they were truly alone.

Will looked up to the heavens, impatient for Tur-tle's news. The moon and stars were shrouded in a thick cloud bank. By morning there'd be a covering of snow. The sounds of drunken celebration from the great hall were smothered by the night and heavy air.

"All right," said Turtle, returning. "We're alone for now."

"Where *is* she?"

"In Somerset, with her uncle, the archbishop of Wells."

"And she took the children and all her ladies?"

"She didn't want any to remain to bear the earl's wrath."

"What has happened that she fears the earl now?" asked Will.

"I am not privy to that," said Turtle.

There was no reason for Turtle to know all of Lady Elaine's secrets. But Will felt that Turtle was holding something back. He tried again.

"But why did she take all the children? Can a lady leave her husband and take his son?"

"Well, *she* did," said Turtle. "And are you not her friend to wish her well away from this place?"

Of course he was her friend. He wanted her safe. But a lady should not run away.

"Why didn't she tell me?"

"She didn't want you giving her away."

"I would never betray my lady to the earl!" said Will.

"Not knowingly," said Turtle. He put a hand on Will's shoulder. "It was her way of protecting you."

Will shrugged off Turtle's hand. He stomped over to the wall and looked out at the shadow of Oxford town. Protected! Like a babe. Lady Elaine hadn't that much faith in him after all, and now she was gone. D'Artois was dead. And John was half what he'd been when they set out for Lincoln. Why had she gone? She had wanted to protect Will and John and hadn't succeeded. Was her leaving another way to protect them? Or did *she* need the greater protection of the archbishop?

"Was this the reward the earl said awaited me at Oxford?" asked Will.

"I don't know the earl's mind," said Turtle. "Word would have reached him at Lincoln that Lady Elaine had gone. But his 'reward' may be a different matter."

Will sighed. He suddenly felt so weary. He had dreaded the return to Oxford, dreaded seeing his lady's disappointment. But this was worse — much worse.

"Go to your bed," said Turtle. "Perhaps daylight will reveal the earl's intentions."

"First I'll look in on John," said Will. "He may need a draught to help him sleep."

"I would not have him sleep too soundly in this place," said Turtle.

Many of the wounded remained at Lincoln to gather strength. Those who returned to Oxford were put in a chamber off the chapel, where the infirmarer and two lay brothers from the Priory of Osney tended them. Will entered the murky room lit by one smoking torch. The lay brothers dozed on benches and two score of wounded lay on pallets, lined up in neat rows.

John was wide awake.

"Are you in pain?" asked Will.

"I'm all right," said John. "Just not ready for sleep."

"Would you like me to prepare you a draught?"

"No," said John. "I need what wits I have left. But stay a moment, Will."

157

John looked around, then drew Will close and whispered in his ear.

"Get word to Father. I must leave Oxford Castle."

For the first time ever, he saw fear in John's eyes. Will nodded. Somehow, he'd get a message to Sir John.

"I'll bide here a while," said Will. "I'm not sleepy either. But you must rest. No more talking."

John smiled and the lines of worry and fear on his face softened. Within seconds he was asleep.

Will sat on the cold floor, watching John sleep through half the night. They both had reason to fear at Oxford Castle. It wouldn't take much to snuff out either of them. Will had been too worried about John to think of his own safety. But once John was out of the way, surely the earl would quickly rid himself of the younger Belet. Or perhaps Earl Aubrey would dispose of Will first. Then it would be even simpler to finish off John. There was too much to worry about. First he must get word to Sir John. Will's head grew so heavy. And yet, his worries kept him wakeful. After the midnight service one of the monks tried to shoo him away. But, as much as he ached for his own bed, Will could not leave John alone. At last Turtle came, promising to keep watch for him. Will stumbled to the barracks and fell onto his cot, asleep.

With the dawn, the old routines of the castle began again. But all was different. Squire Oderic replaced

Squat Wat. He was known to be strict and a hard taskmaster, but he took no pleasure in meanness. The foulest chores were shared out equally among the pages. Will and Turtle were freed at last from the piss pots. As the nursery was empty, Will was sent to help out the infirmarer. Turtle came with him. As ever he was Will's shadow, but Will no longer minded.

Brother Jocelyn, the infirmarer, didn't show much pleasure when they reported to him.

"Men I needed," he said. "Men with experience, and I am sent boys!"

"Please, sir," said Turtle.

Unbidden, Turtle was speaking! Will could hardly believe it.

"What is it?" asked Brother Jocelyn.

"This is the one they call Rabbit," said Turtle.

Rabbit! Why on earth did he have to tell the infirmarer *that?* Will glared at Turtle, who paid him no mind.

"Indeed," said Brother Jocelyn, without a laugh or snicker. He shifted the weight of his gaze to Will. It was terribly uncomfortable, having those wintry gray eyes on him. They seemed to see every flaw in his body and soul.

"Well, Rabbit," said Brother Jocelyn, his voice warmer than before. "There is much to do. Turtle, you follow Brother Jason. He will show you your tasks. Rabbit, you come with me."

159

All the dressings on the wounds needed to be changed. Brother Jocelyn showed Will how it was to be done. He had great skill and gentleness. Will followed his every move, trying to equal Brother Jocelyn's deftness and care. Six of the men had come down with the wound fever. Brother Jocelyn showed Will his preparation of black hellebore to draw out the ill humors of the wounds. Then he bid Will recreate his recipe, all the while studying him with those stern, all-seeing eyes.

"Yes, yes, Rabbit, that is the way." His voice gentled as the morning passed. Will felt slightly less nervous. But the infirmarer could spy out the slightest mistake, so Will took great pains not to err.

John seemed more himself in the daylight, though Will had little chance to speak with him. They worked through the long morning. At noon, Brother Jocelyn had trays of food sent from the kitchen. With his lady gone, there was no need for her cupbearer in the great hall. Brother Jocelyn blessed their bread, and they sat at a makeshift table in a small closet off the main chamber to eat.

"Are you the two night watchers my lay brothers could not be rid of?" asked the infirmarer.

"Yes, sir," said Will. "You see, my brother —" What could he tell Brother Jocelyn? That John, with good reason, feared for his life? No. He couldn't say that. Those winter eyes were heavy upon him.

160

"Well, you can't be up half the night and still be of use to me in the morning," said Brother Jocelyn. "Tell Squire Oderic I need you to sleep here."

He looked from Turtle to Will. "And you may place your pallets on either side of John Belet, if that will get you all to sleep through the night."

"Thank you, sir," said Will. That was a burden gone. But there would still be many hours in the day that they'd not be able to protect John. He must get word to Sir John, and soon. Could he ask the infirmarer to send a message? No, the earl would know of it. He'd have to find another way.

In the afternoon, Will and Turtle were sent to train with the other pages. It was good to be out in the cold after the close air of the sick room. New snow had painted the yard white and clean.

It was a game to train for war, a game that should be played in earnest. There was no time on the battlefield for indecision — no time to be a rabbit. They began with wrestling to warm them. Will thought of the life-and-death struggles he'd seen at Lincoln. He grappled with his partner, Roger, the memory of real fighting coursing through his limbs. He fought as he would have fought John's assassins had he been able.

"Rabbit, RABBIT! Enough!" said the squire, pulling Will off his partner.

Roger lay in the snow bloodied and spent. No one was laughing. The other pages backed away from

161

Will with fear and respect in their eyes. Someone helped Roger get up. Turtle clapped a hand on Will's shoulder.

"Master William," he said, rubbing Will's shoulder. "Will, calm yourself."

Will shuddered and the fury left him.

Then Squire Oderic had them line up with short bows and long. They loosed their bolts on the targets at the far end of the field. His arrows found their mark, most of them. But Will felt a tightness in his bow arm. He was tense, waiting for something, not knowing what.

"Rabbit, steady your gaze, and your arrows will fly true," said Squire Oderic.

"Yes, sir," said Will. He bent to fix another arrow in his bow.

Rabbit, Rabbit, Rabbit. Spoken without meanness or ridicule, unlike Squat Wat or d'Artois. No one had teased him or spoken harshly. But that was what he waited for — the sour remark, the barbed jest. Squire Wat, his constant foe, and d'Artois, his foe *and* protector, both were gone.

XVII.
Help

"Steady on," said Turtle.

Will caught himself in time. He'd nearly swooned on top of Geoffrey of Farnham. Three days had passed since their return to Oxford, and for three days he'd hardly slept. In spite of Brother Jocelyn's kindly intentions, having a pallet next to John did not allow him to rest easy. At night he worried. He hadn't yet worked out a plan to get a message to Sir John. He still didn't know what the earl had in store for him. He kept thinking that if only Lady Elaine had stayed in Oxford, she would know what to do. She would have helped him. But it wasn't for the lady to solve *his* problems. She had troubles enough of her own. And though the battlefield was far behind him, Will remembered it too well, especially at night.

The only time he felt freed from his worries was on the training field. His lifelong dream of knighthood had been tarnished by the reality of the battle of Lincoln. He'd seen too much in the fighting that had little to do with valor, glory, or the tales of King Arthur. And yet, it was what belonged to him. Even his uncle's treachery could not destroy his dream of chivalry. Will was more determined than ever to go beyond the rabbit and become a true knight.

"You should go to Wallingford and let Lady Margaret fatten you up," said Turtle. "If you eat, you'll sleep and leave off fainting like a woman."

"Wallingford!" said Will. "You're absolutely right."

Why hadn't he thought of Wallingford before? Sir Brian would send word to Blindley Heath for him. But how and when could he go? From dawn through the noon dinner he worked in the sick room. Afternoon to vespers he trained with the other pages. There was no time he wouldn't be missed. He'd have to ask permission of Brother Jocelyn and leave John unattended.

Will waited until he was alone with the infirmarer.

"Sir," said Will. "May I have your leave to ride to Wallingford?"

"I cannot spare you here, Rabbit. Surely you can see that."

Brother Jocelyn put down the mortar and pestle and looked closely at Will.

"This has some import for you, doesn't it?"

"Yes, sir, I must go. I —"

"No, don't tell me," said Brother Jocelyn. "I think it best that I know little of your errand. I will send word to Squire Oderic that I have need of Lady Margaret's supply of dittany, and ask that he excuse you and Turtle this afternoon."

"Thank you, sir," said Will. Now he must make some arrangement for John's safety. "Brother Jocelyn . . ."

"What, Rabbit?"

"It's my brother . . ."

"John Belet will be in my care until you return," said Brother Jocelyn. "Go with an easy mind."

"Thank you, sir, I will." Will bowed deeply.

When food was brought from the kitchen, Will and Turtle wrapped bread and hard cheese in napkins and went to the stables to saddle their horses. Will's little mare snorted a greeting and greedily ate the carrot he'd brought for her.

They rode hard to Wallingford and were soon crossing the gatehouse into the bailey. They were brought to the hall, where Sir Brian sat over the bones and scraps of dinner, talking with his men.

"Greetings, Master Will!" shouted Sir Brian. "Come sit you here with me."

Room was made for Will at the head table. Will blushed, feeling the eyes of Sir Brian's men on him. They must wonder why a boy was given such an honor.

"Thank you, Sir Brian," said Will. "I mayn't stay but a short time. I am needed back at Oxford Castle."

"Aye, that you may carry on with your good work," said Sir Brian. "But you must eat, while you tell me of your errand. You are even paler now than you were at Lincoln. Drink some ale."

A place was made for Turtle among the knights at the side table. While Sir Brian ordered them food and drink, Will looked around for sign of Edith. She might be in the solar or out running wild in the snowy fields.

A page brought Will a pewter cup and a trencher heaped with venison and spiced apples.

"What brings you to us?" asked Sir Brian.

"I beg a favor of Lady Margaret from Brother Jocelyn, the infirmarer," said Will, loudly. And dropping his voice, "And a favor of Sir Brian for the Belets of Blindley Heath."

Sir Brian nodded. "How fares my squire, Taroc?"

"It goes well with him. His wound heals and soon he'll be back in your service."

"And John Belet?" asked Sir Brian, his question only loud enough for Will to hear.

Will shook his head.

"Once you've had your fill, lad, go to Lady Margaret in the solar. She will fix you up with *all* that you need. Ask her for anything, anything for the son of the most valiant Sir John Belet," said Sir Brian, patting Will's hand. "Now eat!"

He seemed to know more than Will had told him. And praising Sir John before his men, he showed Will great favor — almost too much for one who owed fealty to the earl of Oxford. Will speared a morsel of meat with his knife. For the first time since Twelfth

166

Night, food tasted good. He ate well and listened to the men talk of Empress Matilda, who was now in London Town to gain its support.

"The empress spoils all that we've won for her with her haughty ways," said one of Sir Brian's knights.

"It does look badly," said Sir Brian, shaking his head. "The people of London will not put up with an arrogant woman. Even King Stephen knew to mind his manners with the Lord High Mayor of London Town."

"They say she *demands* a huge sum of money from the burghers. And that those who first welcomed her into London are now plotting to be done with her."

"Aye, Empress Matilda's ways are unseemly for a gentlewoman and the Lady of England," said Sir Brian, and he drained his cup.

There was a grumble of assent.

Will thought of all those dead at Lincoln. They had won a great battle for the empress. Would that she did not lose them the war. Will once again lost his stomach. He looked to Turtle, who nodded.

"Sir Brian," said Will, "thank you for your gracious hall. I beg your leave to seek Lady Margaret."

"You are welcome to our bounty and our help," said Sir Brian, and he clasped Will's hand.

Will and Turtle climbed the steep stairs to the solar.

"Will! Turtle!" said Edith, knocking over her stool as she rose to greet them.

Her hair was drawn up in a coif, and in spite of

upending the stool, she looked more a lady than she had at the Christmas feasts.

"Welcome, Master Will," said Lady Margaret from her loom. "I'm glad you are able to visit. Bring Edith's stool and sit by me."

"I've come on an errand for Brother Jocelyn," he said. "Have you any white dittany to spare? It would greatly help the fevered men."

"Certainly," said Lady Margaret. "Edith, fetch my chest of medicines."

"All right," said Edith. "But don't talk about anything interesting until I'm back. Master Torrence, will you help me? The chest is heavy."

Turtle silently followed her out of the room. When they had gone, Will spoke into Lady Margaret's ear.

"And I would ask a favor of you," he whispered.

Lady Margaret inclined her head and carried on with her weaving, creating enough clatter to cover Will's words.

"My brother, John, must return to Blindley Heath. I . . . I fear . . . I must send word to my father to come for him."

Lady Margaret nodded. She stilled the loom as Edith returned with Turtle, carrying the large wooden chest.

"Hurry with this," said Edith. "And come see the puppies. There are two for you to name."

"I've not quite finished with Master Will," said Lady Margaret, laughing. "I want him to write a word to Simon."

She rose from her loom and led Will to her closet in a far corner of the solar. Edith followed with Turtle in tow. Lady Margaret brought Will a writing box, pen, and sheet of parchment.

Edith lit a torch and set it in the wall near Will.

"Tell Simon to draw me a picture of Godstone," she said. "And tell him —"

"Edith," said Lady Margaret. "Give Will some peace."

"Sorry," said Edith, and she stepped back into the shadows.

Now that he had his chance, will wasn't sure what to write. He must say enough to bring Sir John quickly to Oxford, but not enough to cause more trouble should the letter fall into the wrong hands. It would ill repay the Fitz Counts if their help caused them woe. He dipped the pen in ink and began.

Sir John Belet of Blindley Heath, Surrey.

Most honored Father,

Please come to Oxford as soon as you're able. John is not well and needs you.

Your obedient son,
Will

Will underlined "needs," sighed deeply, and sealed the letter with hot red wax.

Before Edith could claim him, Lady Margaret stepped forward and took the sealed letter. At the same time she drew a letter from her sleeve and handed it to Will. It had Lady Elaine's seal on it.

"Read it in private," whispered Lady Margaret, "and then destroy it."

He wanted to tear off the seal but instead, he tucked the letter inside his tunic with shaking hands.

"Now he's mine!" said Edith. "Master Torrence, you come too."

Before she dragged him down the stairs, Will turned back to Lady Margaret.

"My thanks to you and Sir Brian."

"The good will between our families goes back to before Duke William," said Lady Margaret. "We will do all we can to help."

Will bowed and followed Edith and Turtle down the stairs. The hall was quiet except for two hounds gnawing on bones.

"The puppies are in here most of the time," said Edith, going to the butler's closet. "It keeps them from harm's way. But if you like, we can take them outside for a romp."

"We can't stay long," said Will. "I wish we could. I wish there was time for skating."

Edith shrugged.

"Can't be helped," she said. "Next time."

She opened the door to the closet and immediately they were set upon by six yipping pups.

"Father says they are the best hunters he's ever bred."

Edith knelt and let the pups climb on her gown and kiss her with their pink, wet tongues. They were bigger than Will had expected. But time had passed since his first visit to Wallingford, and so much had happened.

"Here," said Edith. She held up two sleek-furred, squirming pups, a white one splashed with black flecks, the other tawny brown. "What will you call these two?"

Will knelt on the rushes. The pups were wildly wagging from their fat little tails to their slurping tickling tongues. Will laughed and handed the speckled one to Turtle.

"I can only manage one," he said.

"Father said you saved many men with your doctoring," said Edith. "He is proud to call you friend. These pups are his gift to you."

Will felt the blood rushing to his face.

"But it is too much," said Will. "I can't —"

"For now we'll keep them for you," said Edith. "But all the same, they are yours."

Will had never had a dog to call his own. And now he had two. It was too much. He looked at Turtle, who was nuzzling the speckled one.

"Sir Brian mustn't take offense," said Will to Edith.

"Two dogs are too many for me. The speckled white I give to Turtle."

Turtle looked at Will, startled. For once Will had caught him off guard. And then, for the very first time, Turtle smiled a real smile.

"The names?" asked Edith.

Turtle held up his wriggling pup.

"Such a pretty little maiden," he said. "A bit wild. But I can imagine where that comes from." Turtle glanced sideways at Edith, and Will laughed.

"Maiden," said Turtle. "Sweet Maiden it is."

Edith narrowed her eyes and looked to Will. He was still laughing, but her look stifled him.

"Well, ahem," said Will. "This little brute shall be a great leader among dogs." He held the soft creature aloft. "I name you Uther Pendragon."

The puppy chose that moment to release a stream of urine. Will nearly dropped him.

"Ha!" said Turtle. "Already he shows his mettle!"

They all laughed. Edith brought Will a cloth to dry his splashed tunic. And then it was time to go.

They found Sir Brian in the bailey. Will knelt before him.

You have honored me grandly with your gift," said Will. "May I be worthy of it."

Sir Brian smiled and bid him rise.

"For now Edith will take charge of the pups," he said. "Come as often as you can to keep her in check or your dogs will be good for nothing but mischief."

Their horses were ready for the race back to Oxford Castle. All the long cold ride Will held onto the warm memory of the squirming pup, though the letter in his tunic nearly burned. If they weren't going at such a pace, he'd have read it while they rode. No. He'd have to wait for a time all to himself. His lady had left but hadn't forgotten him. The words of her hand were there, tucked against his heart. No matter what Lady Margaret had said, he could never destroy Lady Elaine's letter.

John was sitting up when Will returned. He had fared well under Brother Jocelyn's care, though he seemed much relieved to see Will. Will whispered in his ear, "Sir Brian is sending word to Blindley Heath."

John lay back on his cot and smiled.

"Then all will be well," he said.

It wasn't until late that night that Will had a chance to think more of Wallingford, Sir John, or Lady Elaine. When all men slept he left his cot to read Lady Elaine's letter by the red glow of smoldering embers.

Master William Belet

My Dear Will,

Forgive me for leaving without saying good-bye. Having lost the good will of my lord, I can no longer stay in Oxford. I hope by my leaving to provide my cousin's sons with a safer position in Oxford Castle. I cannot promise it, but I think the earl will now deal fairly with the Belets of Blindley Heath. And yet you must be on your guard. Beware the earl.

If ever you need my help, Lady Margaret will send me word.

As always, your most loving,
Lady Elaine

Will's heart was pounding as he refolded the letter. No wonder Lady Margaret had told him to burn it. If this letter should fall into the earl's hands . . . Will shuddered and dropped the letter onto the glowing embers. It flamed quickly and soon was gone to ashes — the letter he'd hoped to save and cherish. But he could not risk his lady's welfare for his own fancies. What did she mean, that her absence would make him and John safer at Oxford? Will returned to his cot as stealthily as he'd left it. Had he been right to send for Sir John? Would it offend the earl, and put them all in more danger?

At last Will slept, but he did not rest easy.

XVIII.
Staying On

Will waited daily for some news of Sir John, even though it would have taken several days for messengers to go to Blindley Heath and back. Perhaps Sir John couldn't send a message. What if he wasn't at Blindley Heath to receive Will's letter? What would Lady Alice make of it? His mother already had enough to fret her. John seemed to grow calmer with each passing day, but Will became more and more nervous. He dared not meet the eye of the earl, lest he betray Lady Elaine's secrets or his own.

And then, ten days after Will's visit to Wallingford, Sir John rode into Oxford Castle with Peter of Redvers and a well-armed escort. Will was so glad to see his father, he nearly wept. John, too, was much improved by the arrival of Sir John. He was at once more alert and at ease than he'd been since before the battle at Lincoln.

The earl expressed no surprise at Sir John's coming.

175

Indeed, he might have been the author of Sir John's summons, he seemed so in favor of the plan to remove John to Blindley Heath. For his part, Sir John showed no amazement that Lady Elaine was gone from Oxford Castle. Had she sent him word of her leaving? Had the earl learned of Will's letter to Blindley Heath? Or were they both so schooled in disguising their emotions that nothing could move them?

Will had only one private moment with Sir John during his two days at Oxford. The wounded men were all much improved, and Brother Jocelyn had spared Will to go hawking with Sir John and the earl's men. A gentle wind stirred the trees, hinting of the spring to come. Soon the villeins would be plowing the fields. Here and there the green shoots of snowdrops poked through the winter carpet of dead leaves.

Sir John led Will away from the other knights. They spoke quickly and in whispers.

"You could return to Blindley Heath with me," said Sir John.

He could? He could! It would be so easy to go home, to give up all the worries and fears he'd found at Oxford. But if he left Oxford that was what he'd be doing — giving up. For the long years of his sickness, and even before that, his dream was of becoming a knight. How could he betray that dream? He would stay in spite of the earl. He would give that proof of his fortitude to Lady Elaine.

"I'd lose my chance for knighthood if I left Oxford," said Will.

"There are other roads besides Oxford that lead in that direction," said Sir John.

"Wouldn't it be an open breach with the earl if I left?" asked Will.

Sir John was silent a moment. He cleared his throat.

"It would be best if you stayed," he said. "And I believe that it will be safe here, now."

"Lady Elaine said as much in her letter," said Will.

"She did?" said Sir John.

Will felt himself blushing.

"Yes," said Will. "And I've not understood it."

Sir John leaned over his horse and spoke in Will's ear.

"As you are in the earl's keeping, the earl's sons are in the care of the archbishop of Wells."

"They're hostages?" asked Will.

"Shhh!"

"But Lady Elaine would never let anyone come to harm," said Will.

"Of course not," said Sir John. "Yet the earl is not so sure of her because *he* wouldn't hesitate to harm anybody to get what he wanted."

So Earl Aubrey was tricked by his own treacherous ways.

"Will," said Sir John, his voice becoming very gentle. "What can you tell me of d'Artois? John's story was muddled."

Though Will had known this moment would come, he still wasn't prepared to tell of the battle of Lincoln. Tears pricked his eyes, and he blinked them away. Sir John nodded encouragement. Will swallowed and began.

"Four yeomen attacked John. As d'Artois was defending him, a knight rode up and dealt him a mortal blow. I should have been with them from the first. I should have done something. Lady Elaine told me to watch out for John. I could have helped, and d'Artois would still be alive."

"But you did help," said Sir John. He put a heavy hand on Will's shoulder. "You and Torrence of Cornwall *saved* John. Lady Elaine did not mean for you to have fought in the battle. You did more than could have been expected of a boy. I am proud to have you for a son."

Will heard his father's words and was grateful. But they didn't change anything. The battle at Lincoln had shown him to be a rabbit. Nothing could change that.

The next day John went home to Blindley Heath and Will stayed on at Oxford. He sent a long letter to Lady Alice, mostly thanking her for the skills she'd taught him speaking little of the woe he'd seen. It might be a long time before he'd be able to send word to her again. Shortly after that, Earl Aubrey took nearly all his men to make a round of visits and inspections of his holdings in the Marches. The household went with him, as well — cooks, clerks, huntsmen, hounds, and hawks — in a caravan that made the baggage train for the Lincoln battle seem a paltry thing.

Will and Turtle were left with the small garrison that guarded Oxford Castle. The wounded from the Lincoln battle no longer needed constant care, so Brother Jocelyn returned to the Priory of Osney.

They were free to resume their page duties, but with the castle empty of its lord and lady, there was little for a page to do. It was shameful to be left behind. All the other boys had gone with Earl Aubrey. Will and Turtle were left with the villeins and servants. There were still daily training sessions in the yard, run by one of the squires on guard. Will worked hard. But the fury that had driven him when he first returned from Lincoln was mostly spent. He was able to concentrate more on his skills. He found that he could compensate for his lack of strength by the way he held the broadsword and his timing when he swung it. When he loosed a bolt at the target, he could almost hear d'Artois faulting his aim. He'd listen to that phantom voice, and the next arrow would find its mark.

He and Turtle were often able to ride to Wallingford. The days grew longer and warmer. Spring spread a carpet of tender green over the land. They chased the growing puppies over the flowering hills and through the scented copses of Wallingford. Uther was growing to fit his illustrious name and showed the speed and strength he'd need for the hunt. Maiden had boundless energy, much like her namesake. Edith ran as free as the pups, often ahead of them all in spite of Dame Emma's scoldings.

They were always welcomed at Sir Brian's hall, where they'd linger to hear the news of the land. One afternoon in May, Sir Gregory of Sherborne, come from the West Country, was telling of the newest turn of events.

"The bishop of Winchester, King Stephen's *own* brother, has denied the king and given the Empress Matilda and Earl Robert the city of Winchester!"

Winchester was the treasury and royal seat of all the kings of England! If Matilda held Winchester she was in effect regent of England.

"Quite a stroke for the empress and young Lord Henry," said Sir Brian. "Imagine, the king's brother turning against him!"

"The first thing she does, once inside the castle, is demand the king's crown."

Sir Brian laughed and shook his head.

"Our lady loses not a moment!"

"Ah, but then my tale takes a bad turn," said Sir Gregory. "Comes Stephen's Queen Maude with a great levy, and besieges the city!"

This was the first Will had heard of Queen Maude.

She sounded every bit as formidable as the empress.

"How goes it now?" asked Sir Brian.

"Gravely," said Sir Gregory. "The earl of Chester forgets the debt he owes Earl Robert and makes no move to help. Earl Aubrey, as you know, is fighting the border Scots for his demesnes in Cumberland."

Sir Gregory drew a breath, and all were silent, waiting for what he'd next say.

Sir Brian gave Will a deep look. Earl Aubrey wouldn't risk his own lands to aid the Lady of England.

"I hear that the earl of Surrey is now raising a levy to go to Winchester to free Matilda."

Sir Brian looked again to Will. Yes, he'd understood. Sir John would ride with the lords of Surrey to fight under the earl's banner.

"Then I will go with them!" said Sir Brian, banging the table with his fist.

That's what Will wanted to say and do. But he couldn't leave Oxford without Earl Aubrey's command. And the earl had left him in the empty castle unable to *do* anything. Will finally understood the reward the earl had promised him at Lincoln. This was it! Will wouldn't be harmed; he wouldn't be helped; he'd be left behind, perhaps forever. The earl didn't have to advance Will. He could leave him a page or a squire until he was a graybeard. Will could be kept more useless than the lowest serf.

Within a week, Sir Brian and most of his men left

to join the forces of Surrey. And soon after, Lady Margaret took Edith and her ladies on a retreat to Woburn Abbey, which was felt to be safer than remaining with a small guard at Wallingford.

If Will had gone home to Blindley Heath when his father offered it, he'd now be riding west with Sir John and the lords of Surrey. Even if he couldn't fight, he could help doctor the wounded, groom the horses, or help the cook. Anything would be better than the long, empty summer ahead.

If only Edith had stayed. Poor Edith. Shut up in Woburn Abbey, it would be a hard summer for her, too. She tried to make light of it when she'd said good-bye.

"Oh, I shall be a devilment for the good sisters," she said. "Perhaps they'll ask us to leave."

She'd said it laughing, but her eyes were already shadowed by the high walls of the abbey.

With Edith gone, only Turtle and the dogs were left. Maiden and Uther Pendragon came to live at Oxford. Uther slept at the foot of Will's cot, though often Will woke at night with Uther nestled warm against him. It was foolishness to share his bed with a dog. But Will never made him leave. Whatever Lady Elaine's arrangement with the earl, Will slept sounder with Uther by his side.

When time hung too heavily at Oxford, Will went to Brother Jocelyn at the priory. The infirmarer was always glad of an extra hand and taught Will many things that summer. When there wasn't a patient in need, Brother Jocelyn set Will to studying the massive calf-bound and gilt herbal that each infirmarer had added to since the founding of the abbey. Studying the learned text encouraged Will to return to his Latin lessons, for much in the herbal was difficult for him to understand.

Turtle continued to trail Will, although his attention seemed focused on training Maiden and the bright-colored balls he constantly juggled. Turtle moved very little, but the balls, in ever increasing numbers, flew round and round. Round and round.

Day followed stifling day to the drone of bees and the steady chop-chop of hoe and mattock as the villeins worked the gardens and fields. Will swam through the languid days of July and August with Uther panting at his heels. He trained as hard as ever, but he might as well have been sleeping all that long summer. The only thing that roused him was the news he'd find at the Priory of Osney.

Mendicant friars, messengers for the great lords of England, knights, ladies and pilgrims young and old stopped at the abbey on their journeys. Each had a tale to tell. Brother Jocelyn, with much prodding, would sometimes share this news with Will. But his best source was Brother Theodore, who waited on the abbot's table and saved up every scrap of information that came his way.

"The lady of Leicester is refusing to remarry in

spite of the king's orders. The lord who was promised her hand and *lands* has brought it to the bishop. And he'll have to —"

"What about Winchester?" asked Will. "What news of there?"

"None good," said Theodore. "They say the city is starving. They've eaten all the dogs and started on the horses."

Will patted Uther's head.

"Some supplies are smuggled in under cover of night. But it isn't enough."

Another day in early August the news was more encouraging.

"Earl Aubrey de Vere is victorious in Cumberland. He rides south to aid the empress and Earl Robert."

But by Lammas Day, in mid-August, the wheel of fortune had turned once again.

"Queen Maude has captured Earl Robert of Gloucester!" Brother Theodore was breathless.

"What! Has Winchester been taken by Queen Maude's levy?"

"Nay. Empress Matilda and Earl Robert were trying to make their escape from the starving city." Theodore was shaking as he spoke. "Earl Robert sacrificed himself that the empress might get away."

And that ended the advantage for Empress Matilda and Lord Henry. The wisest lords of the land came together to negotiate the exchange of prisoners. Both

184

King Stephen and Earl Robert were freed. With King Stephen at large, the empress had lost her best chance.

All the gains from the battle of Lincoln, and all the sacrifices, had come to naught. For as long as Stephen wore the crown, the people of England were lost.

Sir John sent a message to Will that he was well and returning to Surrey. There was no word from Somerset.

It seemed that summer would never end. And then one September day a cool wind blew in from the West. With it came startling news. Earl Aubrey de Vere was returning to Oxford, bringing with him Empress Matilda!

XIX.
Mummers

The household returned to Oxford five days before the earl to ready the castle for the arrival of the empress. Will was caught up in the frenzy of preparations, once again page to Aubrey de Vere. New rushes were laid throughout the castle. Carpets were beaten in the yard and rehung on newly whitewashed walls. All that was precious returned to Oxford Castle. The ghostly halls of the long, dusty summer rang with life.

It was a relief to waken from his summer's slumber and once again be caught up in the excitement of the grand castle, to feel part of the great events of England. But all the frenzy meant the return of Aubrey de Vere. No doubt the earl still felt enmity toward the house of Belet. No doubt he still desired Blindley Heath. And Will *did* doubt that Lady Elaine's stay in Somerset still had the power to restrain the earl of Oxford. Not that Will could do anything but fulfill his duties and worry. It was just as well there was little time for worry.

"Rabbit! To the kitchen! To the tower! To the Gardens!" . . . all day long and into the night, so that Will heard orders shouted in his dreams. And just as often in those dreams he'd hear a warning voice very like that of d'Artois: "Rabbit, watch your back! The earl returns — beware!"

An apartment was prepared for the empress in what had been Lady Elaine's chamber. Lady Marle had come with the baggage to make sure everything was properly arranged.

"No! No! NO!" said Lady Marle. "You've got the bed hangings upside down!"

Turtle's eyes flickered briefly. It wasn't really fair of him to tease Lady Marle. She was in a state of nerves to begin with. The slightest mishap had her in tears. The empress's furnishings were far grander than anything Will had ever seen before. Yet when the rooms were arranged to Lady Marle's satisfaction, they looked jumbled and ugly.

Will often stopped midtask to remind himself that soon the Lady of England would be at Oxford Castle. Perhaps he might find a way to do her some special service. He could find some small way to serve England in helping his lady liege. At least he now had a role. This time he wasn't to be left behind or cut off from the events of the world. The excitement swirled around and washed over him. The empress was coming!

Will worked side by side with the other pages. All had returned except Hubert, who was buried in the north. Though nothing was said about it to Will, by their serious looks it was clear that now all the pages had had their training in blood. The other boys kept to themselves and had little to do with Will. No one even mentioned Maiden or Uther Pendragon. Will could have grown a third arm and no one would have noted it. The barracks were full once again, but Will was more than ever on his own.

The day before the earl was to arrive, Will chanced to be on the battlements when a large, well-armed party approached Oxford Castle under colors Will didn't recognize.

"Who comes?" he asked the duty guard.

"Upon my soul! It is Lady Elaine with the knights of Somerset!"

Will strained his eyes to see. It was true! Ringed by the proud knights on their chargers and her ladies on their dun and gray mounts, she rode a white palfrey. Lady Elaine was draped in a mantle colored the new green of spring. Will stood at the wall, transfixed. She was back! But how was it possible? Hadn't *she* said that she was out of favor with the earl and it was too dangerous? How could she put herself again in his hands? But oh, his heart was glad to see her.

"Don't stand there gawking like a hoddypeak! Alert the castle: Lady Elaine returns!"

Will delayed one moment more, lifting his hand in greeting. And it seemed his lady raised her eyes and saw him.

"GO!" said the guard, and kicked Will.

At first no one believed him. Giselle the cook boxed his ears.

"Don't you be bringing me tales," she said. "What with all I've got to do!"

But by the time Lady Elaine rode through the gatehouse with her escort from Somerset, all the household was out to greet her. The villeins and cotters left off their tasks and poured into the castle yard with the procession to welcome their mistress home.

The knights of Oxford bowed low, while her own knights helped her and her ladies dismount. The children were handed out of the wagon where they had ridden. Servants ran to kiss the hem of Lady Elaine's gown. Uther and Maiden were prancing and yelping with excitement. Even Giselle was on her knees, weeping. Lady Elaine laughed and greeted all by name, petting the ragtag cotters' children who danced circles around her. She seemed untouched by the dust of the road or the fatiguing journey.

With Lady Elaine came the sweetness and beauty of springtime. The haze and dust of late summer was swept away with the hem of her silken skirt. Her return restored the soul of Oxford Castle. All rejoiced to see her, none more than Will. But he worried at what it might cost her.

"Master Will!" she said, drawing near to him.

Will fell to his knees and touched his head to the ground. Now was the moment he'd dreaded since the battle of Lincoln.

"Rise up, my page."

Now he'd have to tell her about d'Artois and how he'd failed her.

"My lady," he said. "Forgive me, d'Artois is —"

"I know, Will," she said. "I know everything. Come to the nursery after vespers and we will talk."

A fragrant breeze stirred the dull September air as the mistress of Oxford Castle led her ladies across the court to the tower.

Lady Elaine had said she knew everything. That evening, as Will climbed the familiar stairs, trailed by Uther, he wondered if, knowing it all, she had forgiven him.

Lady Elaine, her ladies, and the children had been crowded into the nursery. But as Will entered, all was sweet-smelling and orderly. Lady Elaine beckoned him near. She was more like a fairy queen than the first moment he'd seen her, even with the weariness of the journey now upon her.

"Will!" she said. "You've been growing! And look at this fine hunter you have!"

Uther pricked up his ears and looked as noble as his name.

"He is Sir Brian's gift," said Will. "I hope it is all right to keep him here. If not, Sir Brian will keep him for me."

"He gave you the pick of the litter," said Lady Elaine. "Yes, you may keep him. Get Olsen the houndmaster to help you train him."

She looked at Will again and frowned. Will felt the sweat run down his back.

"Milady, forgive me," said Will, and he knelt before her.

"Rise up, Master Will," said Lady Elaine, "and come with me."

She led him to a cramped closet away from the children and ladies and made him sit on a stool opposite her.

"Will," she said, her voice soft and kind. "There is nothing to forgive."

"But d'Artois —" said Will.

"Sir John told me all about it. He said you took d'Artois's death very hard, and blame yourself for it. Only *one* person caused his death, and you know it wasn't you."

Will sighed.

"If the earl is so dangerous, why are you here?" he whispered.

"Because he asked me," said Lady Elaine.

"But —"

"The empress will be here as well," said Lady Elaine. "The earl is intent on winning her favor. He deems it fitting and necessary that his lady wife assist him in making the empress welcome and comfortable. And he has promised me many things in consideration of my help. As long as Her Imperial Highness is here, Earl Aubrey will keep those promises."

It was a dangerous game. And what did Lady Elaine gain by playing it? Yet, if anyone knew the earl, she did. Will only hoped she wasn't being deceived.

"Milady," said Will, "I'm very glad of your return."

"Thank you, Will. Now let's see what can be done about your tunic." And she called Dame Catherine into the closet.

"Dame Catherine, what can we do to make Master Will presentable to the empress?"

Dame Catherine stepped forward, clicking her tongue, and lifted the hem of Will's tunic.

"There's not enough material to let out," she said. "But I can add a length of cloth to hem and cuff."

"That would help," said Lady Elaine. "Could you attend to it now?"

"Certainly, milady. It won't take but a minute to fix him up."

Lady Elaine withdrew to the nursery, and Dame Catherine at once began altering Will's tunic and filling the small closet with her soft, clucking chatter.

"Seems only yesterday, I was stitching up your tunic to keep it from tripping you," said Dame Catherine. "And here I am, not even a year gone by, adding on twice what I'd taken out!"

He had grown! Seems as if he ought to have taken more notice. He'd taken the wadding out of his boots and still they pinched. His sleeves ended nearer his elbows than his wrists. If he gave it a thought, it was that he'd been out too much in sun and rain and ruined his clothes.

"Soon enough it will be Michaelmas and you shall have new tunic and hose," said Dame Catherine.

"I doubt the earl will be so generous to me."

"Oh, I think you'll find the earl most openhanded on his return to Oxford Castle," said Dame Catherine, and her sides shook with laughter.

When Dame Catherine had finished with him it was getting quite late, but Lady Elaine bid him stay a moment by the fire. All the children slept. Dame Catherine and the other ladies had withdrawn to a far corner, allowing Will and Lady Elaine some privacy.

"Your tunic is much improved," said Lady Elaine.

Will bowed.

"It will see you through until Michaelmas."

"Dame Catherine said the earl would be most generous," said Will. "What did she mean?"

"You must wait and see." Lady Elaine smiled, then her face clouded over and she spoke in an urgent whisper. "But generosity or no, do not think the earl is changed, for he is ever the same."

And then she sent Will to find his bed. The morrow would be filled with the arrival of the earl and empress, and there was still much work to do.

They rode side by side into Oxford Castle on shining black chargers. Empress Matilda sat nearly as tall as Earl Aubrey and wore the same cold look. She was not beautiful; her nose and chin were too strong for beauty, although she was fair. But it was easy to see she was the daughter of a great king, an emperor's consort, and that, by right, she was the Queen Mother. She was, indeed, the Lady of England. The noble blood of King Henry coursed through her veins. Her robe, like that of the earl, was of stiff damask, trimmed with vair. The empress wore the imperial purple. When they dismounted and stood for all to pay homage, they could have been the carved figures on the portal of Oxford Cathedral. They were so alike, and so like pillars of stone. Will shuddered, remembering Lady Elaine's words.

Lady Elaine, nearly half their height, was dressed in sky-colored silks. She went forward to greet them, as light and breezy as a cloud, with all her ladies and the earl's children in tow. She curtsied to the ground before the empress.

"Your Imperial Highness has brought Oxford Castle the highest of honors with your gracious presence," said Lady Elaine.

The empress inclined her head ever so slightly.

"Gracious!" whispered Turtle and snorted.

"I am fatigued," said the empress. "Please show me to my chambers."

Lady Elaine hastened to her feet, leading the empress to what had been her own apartment. And though it was her role to serve the empress, her quiet dignity and grace marked *her* as the nobler of the two.

Each day a great feast was given to equal and surpass the festivities of Yuletide. Nobles came to pay homage to Empress Matilda from all over Oxfordshire, Bedfordshire, and Surrey. Sir Brian came the first day and promised to bring Edith for the Michaelmas celebration. Sir John remained at Blindley Heath. And Will was just as glad not to see the empress snub his father as she did the other nobles.

Once again Will was cupbearer to Lady Elaine and so took his place in the great hall behind her chair. She had also chosen Turtle to attend her. He stood near Will, commenting under his breath on all that happened.

"See how the empress holds her nose so high. Do you think she's been served the offal instead of the oranges?"

How could he make fun of the empress? The Lady

of England? But he did mock her, constantly. And Will in spite of himself was often choking with laughter. Lady Elaine thought that he'd caught a cough. When had Turtle become so talkative? So funny? Was it the arrival of the empress? Or had it started during the summer, and Will was only just beginning to notice?

A troupe of Norman mummers were brought from London to entertain. They acted out *The Play of Adam* and miracles of the saints. In between the sacred stories they juggled and joked. Will watched them, breathless. Turtle also seemed caught by their spell. But he neither laughed at the buffoonery nor wept for the Holy Martyrs, as did Will and nearly all the others in the great hall. Turtle studied the players, looking puzzled and serious as if he were learning a new tongue.

The events at Oxford Castle were very much like a mummery. During the long months of spring and summer the stage had been empty of its players. Then suddenly all had returned, with their masks in place, acting out their parts. Lady Elaine did an excellent job of acting the happy wife, betraying neither anger or fear. Would Oxford's play end in tragedy or foolery? Perhaps Turtle, also, saw the events at Oxford Castle as an unfolding drama, or a farce.

Lady Elaine needn't have been concerned how Will might look to the empress, for she never looked at Will nor *anyone* below the rank of earl. She accepted the homage of the lords of the land with curt nods and impatient looks. Once she'd dismissed them, she turned to Earl Aubrey and asked:

"How many knights can he bring me? How much gold?"

This was not the Lady of England Will had looked for . . . had hoped to fight for, even to die for. He couldn't mock her as did Turtle. But it grieved him that this lady seemed so unlike the sovereign Will had dreamed would save England.

The grandest feast of all was planned for Michaelmas, the twenty-ninth of September. It marked the end of harvest, the time of bounty. All accounts were put in order. The rents due Oxford were paid in goods or promised service. And all who served the earl, from lowly cotter to seneschal, were given their wages and gifts from the lord's hand. Largesse was as important as valor. The castle buzzed with speculation. How would Earl Aubrey reward each one for a year's service? Dame Catherine and Lady Elaine had said the earl would be most generous. But then why had they laughed?

Michaelmas dawn, the seneschal handed out a new suit of clothes to each of the pages, even Will. They had new hose, shirts, tunics, and surcoats, all of fine weave. And to mark the feast, each had a richly embroidered collar in the colors of the empress.

Edith and her parents arrived early Michaelmas

morning along with scores of other noble families and villeins from all over the shire. Will slipped out of the kitchen when Giselle wasn't looking to spend a moment at Edith's side. The convent had changed her; her skin was pale and her eyes shadowed.

"Will!" she said. "I'm so glad to see you. Where's Uther? Was he good? Did he miss me?"

"Yes," said Will. They both had missed her. "I'll take you to see him later if I can get away. Uther and Maiden have grown so much you might not know them."

"As much as you?" asked Edith.

Will felt his color rising, and Edith laughed.

They walked around the courtyard, which had been transformed into the likes of St. Giles Fair. Booths were set up, selling pies and ale. Peddlers hawked trinkets. The mummers tumbled and juggled. A trained bear danced with his master. Then Turtle caught up with them with a command from Giselle, and Will had to go back to the kitchens.

The feasting began at midday and lasted into the night. The hall was so crowded, many of the lesser gentry ate in the courtyard, along with the villeins. But no one missed out on any of the marvels. Between each course, exquisite concoctions called subtleties were paraded slowly through the yard and all around the great hall. Even though he'd watched some of them being made, Will was as astonished as the rest.

A marzipan swan, the size of a horse, had been fitted with a mechanical device that made it rise up and flap its wings as if it would take off in flight. Seeing it, Will nearly dropped his ewer of wine. Even the empress seemed to pay attention.

The grandest surprise of all was saved until the very end of the feast. As with the Yule feast, the tables were cleared away, and the benches were pushed to the sides of the hall. The nobles came forward one by one, from least to greatest, to pledge their fealty and receive the earl's gift. Some had new robes or fur-lined mantles, jewels, or fine weapons. The seneschal was given a manor of his own in Cumberland.

And that seemed to be the end of it. But Earl Aubrey held up his hand to the buzzing hall, and Lady Elaine rose to stand at his side.

Perhaps the priest of St. Michael's Church would give one last blessing. But no one came forward. When the hall was absolutely hushed, Earl Aubrey spoke.

"There is one last gift." He turned to face the empress. "To Matilda, Empress of the Holy Roman Empire and Lady of England, I give . . ."

He paused and the hall held its breath.

"I give Oxford Castle!"

And then Will did drop the ewer.

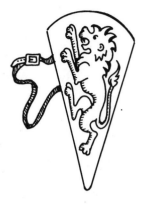

XX.
Plantagenet

Later that night, Will and Turtle were in the butler's pantry polishing the silver and brass.

"He gave away Oxford Castle!" said Will.

"Keep your voice down," said Turtle. "And don't be so impressed."

But he was impressed! The same man who'd been ready to murder his stepsister's sons for a modest de-mesne had just given away Oxford Castle. It was beyond anything Will had ever heard of.

"Surely it was a noble deed," said Will.

Turtle hushed him with a look.

In a moment Alfred entered the pantry. He picked up a silver tray and grunted.

"Make sure you count the cups and ewers before locking up," he said. "Then bring me the keys."

Will and Turtle kept silent until Alfred had crossed the hall and was out of hearing. The great hall was dark except for the smoky light of a few torches and the embers in the grate. A score of knights were sleeping on benches, and many servants were curled up in the rushes with the kitchen dogs. The rhythmic wheeze of the men was lulling Will to sleep. Turtle handed him a ewer and brought him back to his task.

"You, of all people, being taken in by the earl's gesture. One would think you'd had no experience at all in Earl Aubrey's court," said Turtle. "First of all, it is better for the earl to give than wait for the empress to take. Even though it is not really his to give."

It was true that Oxford belonged to the king as did all the great holdings of England. And as his uncle had already sworn allegiance to Empress Matilda, all of Oxford was rightfully hers. But the earl had built Oxford Castle himself.

"Furthermore," said Turtle. "If the empress regains Winchester, she'll have little need of Oxford."

That was true as well. The royal city of Winchester would be much more valuable to the empress than Oxford. Winchester held the crown jewels and the treasury.

"And meanwhile," Turtle continued, "now that Oxford belongs to the empress, she must bear the costs. All in all, I think the earl has done rather well for himself."

There was nothing Will could say to that. He certainly wasn't one to defend Aubrey de Vere. He knew his uncle was wicked, but he hoped that he was not also base, that Aubrey de Vere might prove worthy of his high estate.

To begin with, it mattered little that the castle belonged to Her Imperial Highness. The earl and empress shared the baldaquin in the great hall, though the silk canopy was now scarlet with golden lions rampant. Will and Turtle still served Lady Elaine. And the days followed a familiar pattern of service, work, and study.

Lady Elaine sent Will and Turtle to Wallingford with a letter for Lady Margaret. Edith seemed happy to see Will, and she made much over Uther and Maiden. Then she took up her needlework and sat quietly. She didn't even try to coax them out to the orchards. When Will and Turtle took their leave, she walked them to the stables.

"Is anything wrong?" asked Will.

"No," said Edith. "Everything is as it should be."

She pressed Will's hand and smiled through a veil of sadness.

"But you seem sore troubled," said Will.

"I may not tell you about it now," said Edith. "My life has finally taken a course and I am fool enough to regret it."

Will wished for something to say to cheer her.

"Do not concern yourself for me, Will. All is as it should be."

Will rode away remembering the sorrow in Edith's eyes.

By mid-October things began to change at Oxford Castle. The empress sent for a flock of royal ladies to attend her. Only Lady Marle and Princess Von Holstein shared her chamber. All the other ladies were bedded down with Lady Elaine and the children, where they complained bitterly about their cramped quarters and the lack of respect due them. Lady Elaine was continually trying to settle their squabbles and smooth their ruffled feathers.

Word spread throughout England that the empress was at Oxford. Knights came daily to pledge her their service.

"And get a warm spot to shelter for the winter!" said Turtle, and he laughed at each new arrival.

It did seem that many of the knights were in need. They were tattered and ill-equipped. Even so they were made welcome. It might not be long before King Stephen sought to avenge himself on the empress and every fighting man was an asset. But Turtle disagreed.

"There are too many already," he said. "The castle might support them in an ordinary winter. But all these extra mouths will defeat us in a siege."

Will tried to ignore him. He had too much to think about already. How could he be sure that the earl would keep his pledges to Lady Elaine? And though

John was at Blindley Heath, did that guarantee his safety?

Eighteen new boys came to serve as pages to Empress Matilda. Now Will was one of the senior pages. He was still called Rabbit, though no one seemed to mean any offense by it. The new boys called him "Rabbit, sir," which kept Turtle in stitches.

The barracks were packed with men and boys. Many preferred to sleep in the great hall, where the air didn't smell of feet and there was room to stretch. Uther got into a fight with one of the newcomers' dogs, and had to be chained up. It was the first dog fight, but not the last. The men got into fights, too. There were too many of them with not enough to do.

Wagon loads of grain, vegetables, and fruit came from all over Oxfordshire and as far away as Kent. Even Blindley Heath sent a wagon filled with the autumn harvest. The cellars were loaded with food to support Matilda's garrison over the long winter. Hunting parties went out each morning to bring back game, some for dinner and some to be salted and saved for the thin months. Will tried to calculate if there would be enough food to last out a siege.

Great lords came from all over England and from Normandy and Anjou. They dined privately in the earl's solar or the empress's chamber to work out plans for a spring campaign against King Stephen. Lady Elaine was only included in the war councils if her kinsmen were present. Then Will attended to her. From the little he heard, he had a hard time piecing together their plans. There was much grumbling among the men about these private dinners.

"The empress belongs to her people. She shouldn't hide away in secret conferences."

"She does it to save silver!"

It was true that after Michaelmas, the feasting had diminished. There was always food aplenty, but none of the fabulous dishes or subtleties that had marked the earl's rule. The mummers and dancing bear were sent away and only a harper remained to sweeten the nights with song.

One day Henry Plantagenet, son of the empress and the Duke d'Anjou, thundered through the gatehouse into Oxford Castle guarded by a retinue of young knights. He bore a message from his uncle, Earl Robert of Gloucester. He was at least two years younger than Will, though nearly as tall. Everything about him seemed on fire, from his flame-colored hair to the gilt tips of his boots. Henry fulfilled every scrap of gossip Will had heard about him. He *was* older than his years. And he *was* regal. Turtle kept telling Will not to stare, but he couldn't help it. Though only a boy, Henry was as brilliant as the sun. He reminded Will of how John had looked before he was injured. And unlike his mother, the young lord was interested in everyone he met.

"And who is your cupbearer?" he asked Lady Elaine when they were at dinner in the great hall.

"Master William Belet," said Lady Elaine. "I think you know his father, Sir John."

"Indeed, I've but left his manor a fortnight ago," said Lord Henry. He studied Will with emerald eyes, hard and bright as gemstones. Then he grinned. "Your brother John told me about you, but he was much mistaken. He said you were shorter than me."

"I've grown some since last he saw me," said Will.

"Both you and John do your father proud," said Henry. "He's a lucky man."

He spoke and acted like a man, a noble man. He wasn't cold like his mother or Earl Aubrey, but as warm and friendly as Simon. Will smiled back at him. From what Will had heard this boy was the image of his grandfather, King Henry.

"One day Master Will shall be a most worthy knight," said Lady Elaine. "Meanwhile, he studies hard and has acquired much skill in the healing arts. Already he has given many men back their lives."

Lord Henry held Will in his steady gaze and Will felt his color rising.

"And who is your teacher?" asked Lord Henry.

"Brother Jocelyn of the Priory of Osney has taught me all spring and summer," said Will. "Before that I had the good guidance of my lady mother, and my mistress, Lady Elaine."

"And will you be a physician or a fighter?" asked Lord Henry.

Could there be a choice? Could this boy give Will a chance to choose his life? Someday Lord Henry might well have the power. By right, he should be king.

"I shall be whatever will best serve the empress and England," said Will, with rivulets of sweat running down his back.

"Well spoken, Master Will," said Lord Henry, and he laughed. It was like Edith's laughter, full of mischief and good will. "England shall depend on you."

Will bowed low, trying to hide his glowing face.

"So the realm rests on your shoulders, Master Will," said Turtle later that night, bowing and laughing. "Do you think you can manage it all by yourself?"

Turtle could laugh all he wanted. Will would do or be anything if it would serve Henry Plantagenet. Henry might only be a boy now, but someday he would be the noblest lord of all. He was the master Will had hoped to find at Oxford Castle — the hope of all England. If ever Will could honorably leave Earl Aubrey's service, he would hasten to join Henry Plantagenet.

It was late November, while the earl's villeins were caught up in the work of slaughtering the pigs, that the rumors began. Will listened to all that was said as he moved about the castle from task to task.

"They say King Stephen gathers a huge levy in Essex and will march on Oxford Castle."

"More fool the king, to besiege a castle bursting with a rich harvest!"

Oxford Castle *was* well provisioned. The cellars were filled with grain. Food stores were piled in the stables, the kitchen, the pantries, even the chapel, despite Lady Elaine's protests. There was bounty indeed. There were also *many* mouths to feed, with more men arriving daily, and Will wondered if any amount of stores would suffice.

By early December the rumors were confirmed. Grim-faced messengers rode in from the west. The king's levy was advancing. Villagers poured into Oxford Castle, bringing whatever they could carry and driving cattle and sheep before them to pasture in the outer ward. Huts were hurriedly built all along the curtain wall. Lady Elaine's beautiful garden was soon mired and the fancy flattened trees were pulled down by climbing urchins.

" 'Tis a shame," said Will.

"Never mind the trees," said Lady Elaine. "For we shall see much worse. I think you'd best send Maiden and Uther to Wallingford."

Sir Brian came the next day on an errand for Earl Aubrey, and he left with the dogs. It was hard to send

Uther away. But Will didn't need to be reminded that they'd eaten all the dogs at the siege of Winchester.

"Will Wallingford be all right?" asked Will, as he and Lady Elaine watched Sir Brian ride out of Oxford Castle.

"King Stephen wants the empress," said Lady Elaine. "Wallingford will be safe for now."

"And Oxford?" said Will.

"Oxford is stoutly defended," said Lady Elaine.

"But there are too many in the castle, aren't there?"

"I wish there was time to send the children away to Somerset," she said.

But there wasn't time. Early the next morning the alarm sounded. Oxford Castle was under siege.

XXI.
Besieged

Will stepped out into the frigid yard and breathed deeply. It was good to be free of the stench and crowding of the smoke-filled hall and away from the pretense of the Twelfth Night feast. Soon it would be night. In the dusky light, with the fresh cover of snow, it looked almost peaceful. Will heard laughter from the enemy siege tower just beyond the western wall, and he flinched. There was no peace to be had in a besieged castle.

At first the king's levy numbered some two hundred knights. Turtle said that had they fought the king in the beginning, there never would have been a siege. But the empress insisted on waiting for the levies of Chester and Robert of Gloucester. The days became weeks as more and more standards joined the king. Still there was no sign of either earl. The empress refused to believe that they couldn't or wouldn't come. And so she squandered the castle's reserves.

"It will keep up the morale," she said, and ordered feasts prepared for Advent. The stores might have lasted all winter had they been sensibly rationed at the start.

Even with all the knights who'd flocked to Oxford during the autumn, they couldn't maintain defense of the outer curtain. The king's forces broke through the day after Christmas, and all the cattle and sheep penned in the outer ward were lost to the enemy. And so the rationing began too late. Christmas Day was the last time Will or anyone else except the earl and empress had a full stomach.

Will's stomach growled. Hunger was painful, and there was no physic to help it. Yet Will was one of the lucky ones. Lady Elaine made sure all the children and pages had their fair share of the rations. Not as much could be said for the villeins, who were already starving.

Turtle joined Will, stamping his feet and rubbing his hands.

"Stephen or Matilda," he said. "It makes little difference. We are caught between two devils."

"Quiet!" said Will, looking around to make sure no one was near enough to hear Turtle. There was only Leofric, the reeve's son, and some other boys throwing snowballs. "You'll have us drawn and quartered."

Will and Turtle started cautiously across the snow-covered yard. Will jumped at each little sound, even the soft thuds of snowballs. Who knew when or from where an attack might come?

"Perhaps we should use the inner passageway," said Turtle, "if the Rabbit cannot enjoy one moment of freedom."

Will looked at Turtle and grimaced. It was pointless to worry, to try to be prepared. There could be no preparation for the death that came without warning. Lady Elaine had begged him to avoid the dangers of the open yard, but it was the only place to escape the miserable rat's nest that the grand castle had become.

"Nay," said Will, "never mind the foolish Rabbit's fears. Air and space are worth the risk."

Turtle's mouth curved in a faint smile and they continued silently across the yard. Once they were out in the open where no one was close enough to hear, Will turned and whispered to Turtle.

"King Henry was not a devil!"

"Mayhap some would say he was," said Turtle, his eyes slivered teasingly. "But at least in King Henry's reign the land was whole. Men fought to protect England, not destroy it. For the most part, one could work and pray and live in peace."

"If the succession had not been challenged, there would be peace."

Turtle snorted.

"It's bad luck that the hope of England rests on

milady's shoulders," he said. "Her Imperial Highness can't even rule her own ladies-in-waiting."

"She cannot rule herself!" said Will, in spite of himself. As much as he wanted the empress to win, as much as he believed that King Henry's daughter and grandson must prevail to bring peace to England, Will was beginning to despise Her Imperial Highness.

"I thought you were going to dump the ewer of wine on her when she complained about the mutton," said Turtle, laughing.

"*She* accused Lady Elaine of poor management!"

Turtle shrugged.

"She is the empress."

Empress or not, daughter of King Henry, mother of Lord Henry, it didn't matter. She was petty, selfish, and cruel. How dare she blame Lady Elaine for anything? Lady Elaine scarcely slept, she was so busy keeping the children and spoiled ladies safe and nursing the ever increasing numbers of sick and injured.

Everyone except Empress Matilda and Earl Aubrey lived in total misery. Children wailed; women and grown men wept. Death came daily, snatching away yeoman, mother, child. No one was spared. The fear of death filled each corner of the castle. Every day Will heard a new rumor. The bloody flux broke out, and people said the wells had been poisoned. When a piece of masonry fell from the battlement, word spread through the castle that the wall had been mined and was about to collapse.

On the battlefield the enemy had a man's face. But now the besiegers were hidden behind bunkers, out of bowshot, or in the three monstrous siege towers that faced the western wall. The towers themselves became the enemy. Night and day they spewed forth murderous stones the size of trenchers, or the substance made of naptha, called Greek fire, that burned savagely and couldn't be quenched by water. Rotting carcasses of animals were flung down on the courtyard, a rain of pestilence. Death came from the heavens like a curse. Even the horrors of the battlefield paled in comparison.

Will and Turtle helped Lady Elaine doctor the sick and wounded in the same infirmary where Will had tended the wounded from Lincoln. This was far worse. Cots and pallets filled the room, the corridors, and half the chapel. Many in Will's care were the children of the villeins. The flimsy huts in the courtyard offered little protection from the cold, and none at all from the enemy missiles. Lady Elaine had tried to shelter all the women and children in the great hall, but Empress Matilda wouldn't allow it.

Will sighed. His moment of freedom was over. He and Turtle climbed the stairs to take up their duties in the sick room.

Will had just set a kettle on the brazier to stew

bilberries for those with the flux when he heard the shouts and screaming on the stairs. Will's hand hovered trembling over the kettle. He couldn't move. Had the king's levy broken through the defenses? Will looked to Turtle, who was also frozen in midtask. The door burst open, and Leofric, the reeve's son, was brought into the room, howling. He'd been hit by Greek fire and his leg was burning. It had only been moments since Will and Turtle were in the open yard. Had they walked slower, had the fire been launched sooner, they could be in this boy's place. Lady Elaine arrived, breathless. All the color left her face when she saw Leofric. But she set her mouth in a grim line and helped Will smother the leg with lard-coated wool, while Turtle and the reeve held down the screaming boy. Little that Brother Jocelyn had taught Will could help Leofric.

"Sleep," said Lady Elaine. "We can at least give him sleep."

Will mixed a draught of poppy and mead. They poured it down the boy's throat. And still he howled.

The smell of burned flesh and the wrenching cries sickened Will. Other children were crying now, too, as if the boy's agony had reminded them of their own pain and misery. Why must they suffer? What had little children to do with the battles of lords? Why didn't the knights fight? Knights were trained for battle and hardened to pain. Even now, outnumbered four to one, a fight would be better than this drawn-out waiting for death. King Arthur would have fought. John Belet would have fought rather than watch the men, women, and children of his manor suffer without end. Will would have gladly died in battle instead of spending another night helpless among the sick and dying children.

Turtle let go of the boy and walked to the center of the room, pulling from his sleeve five bright-colored balls. He held them on high for all to see. Then he sent the balls dancing in the air. Round they went, round and round. And as they watched the children quieted. Even Leofric was caught by the magic. Turtle hardly seemed to move. It was as if the balls flew on their own accord. Will had seen Turtle juggle many times before and never seen anything like this. He kept the balls aloft and spinning. No one else moved. One by one the children fell asleep. Then it was over, the moment of magic gone.

At midnight, Will left the stench of the sick room and went up to the western battlements to breathe the cold, sweet air before he slept. Turtle was soon at his side. His shadow. It was hard to imagine that Will needed Turtle's watchful eye, that the earl could be busy plotting against Blindley Heath while Oxford Castle was in such grave danger. But who could fathom the earl? John had been attacked in the midst of battle. Whatever the earl's plans, Will was grateful for Turtle's presence.

"You were the healer tonight," said Will.

Turtle shrugged.

He never gave himself away.

"Who *are* you?" asked Will.

"Who do you think?"

"I think you are a wizard or perhaps a druid," said Will.

"There might be some druid in my blood," said Turtle. "My mother is Prince Llewelyn's kin. And the Welsh still follow the old religion. But juggling isn't magic. It's a skill. You've seen me practice often enough."

"Yes, but —"

"One fine day you will be Sir Rabbit, of the earl's guard, riding from shire to shire, bringing fear and death. And I shall be Turtle the Fool, the bringer of magic and mirth."

"If I ride with Henry Plantagenet," said Will, "I will bring peace to England."

Turtle looked hard at him. "That's a big if," he said. "But miracles have been known to happen, even in England."

Suddenly Turtle's face darkened. He threw back his hood and cocked his head to one side.

"What is it?" asked Will.

"Be still," said Turtle. "Listen."

Sleepy voices of the duty guards, a baby's cry, a woman's song — all muffled by the falling snow.

"I can't hear anything," said Will.

"Listen!"

Then he heard it, almost felt it, a sound as faint as a heartbeat. Clink, clink, pause, clink. It came from the stones in the wall. Clink, clink, pause. Clink.

"What is it?"

Will's own heart was beating wildly against his ribs.

"We must warn the earl," said Turtle. "They're mining the western wall!"

XXII.
Escape

Will and Turtle waited on the eastern battlement, bows at the ready. They'd been there for over an hour with the rest of the castle guard, eyes trained on the western wall. Now the frigid black night was giving way to an ashen dawn. No one spoke. Men shifted uneasily, trying to warm their frozen limbs. The earl's orders were to keep silent and be ready to fire the instant the wall came down.

Will had been staring so hard at it that the wall seemed to waver and dance. That night Turtle and he had made their report to the marshal, who dragged them into the earl's bedchamber that he might hear it directly. Earl Aubrey questioned them minutely and sent the marshal to confirm their story. Turtle was amazingly calm and well spoken before the earl.

When the marshal returned he said, "They speak true, milord. The sappers are hard at work. I think the wall may be down by dawn."

The earl had the empress alerted and gave orders

that woke the castle from its midnight slumber and set in motion its defense. Before Will and Turtle were dismissed, the earl formally thanked them and handed Turtle four silver pennies. Turtle and Will bowed and hurried from the room.

"A handsome reward," said Turtle, handing Will two pennies.

"I can't touch it," whispered Will. "Didn't you see the look in his eye?"

"Venomous, I'd call it," Turtle whispered back. "But the snake's money is good."

Will shivered now, remembering that murderous look, and shivered again from the bitter cold. Turtle had kept the silver.

No matter his wickedness, Aubrey de Vere had readied a skillful defense of the castle.

Archers were stationed in the tower and on the surrounding battlements. Mounted knights had been assembled in the great hall, gatehouse, and kitchens, and heavily armed foot soldiers were hidden in every hut and storeroom around the courtyard. Women, children, and those who could not wield a weapon, were hidden in the storage space beneath the great hall and in the chapel. Will thought he caught a glimpse of Lady Elaine, but the window was quickly boarded up. The empress stood next to the earl, on the gatehouse battlement, dressed as he was in full armor.

And then it came. Will rubbed his eyes again, but the wall did, in truth, move. He drew an arrow from his quiver. The wall creaked and groaned, followed by ear-splitting screeches as stone wrenched against stone. And then it fell. It was the most fearsome thing Will had ever known. He braced himself against a crenelation, the teeth rattling inside his head. The wall roared like a dragon and the stones exploded into the bailey. It was so loud it swallowed up all other sounds. Will could see men shout, but could not hear them. A huge cloud of dust and rubble rose up, monstrous black against the milky sky. Beelzebub had come to Oxford.

As the dust began to settle, the king's men poured through the breach into a ready trap. Earl Aubrey waited until the courtyard was nearly filled with the enemy before signaling the advance.

The doors of the great hall, gatehouse, and kitchen were flung open. The war horns blared. Mounted knights charged into the invaders with swords drawn. Foot soldiers burst from the huts, their pikes and axes flashing. They lunged into battle with murderous cries, rivaling the horns of war and the deafening collapse of the wall. Will shouted, too. Then he loosed an arrow, which brought down a knight wearing the colors of Essex. But before he could feel pride or remorse in the death of his enemy, he'd drawn a second bolt from his quiver, taken aim and shot again.

Hundreds of the king's men perished, cut down by sword and axe, pierced by arrow. When at last the retreat was sounded, the courtyard was mired in slush and blood. Will and Turtle were sent to recover any who might be saved for ransom. Meanwhile the villeins were set to work, throwing the bodies of the enemy outside the walls, and piling up stones to fill in the breach. The king's men fired on them from the siege towers, and scores more were killed.

Now they were worse off than ever before. The western wall could never be properly mended. The enemy's battering rams and mangonels destroyed the patched breach over and over again. The castle was vulnerable to missiles of fire and stone, and raids through the breach. It had been three weeks since Twelfth Night. Three weeks of bitter cold and winter storms. The Thames was frozen solid, and snow lay heavy on the land. The castle was just as cold inside as out. There was so little firewood remaining, only the empress's chamber and the nursery had fires. The food stores were giving out. Sickness spread throughout the castle, along with despair.

"We lost our chance," said Turtle. "The empress should have attacked the king's forces when the western wall fell."

"Torrence!" said Lady Elaine. "I cannot let you speak against the empress." Her eyes flashed. "Even if your words are true."

Turtle laughed and so did Will, though it made him nervous. Men were hanged for less. They were in the nursery closet, with the sleeping children and Dame Catherine guarding the door. Since Lady Elaine's return to Oxford Castle, she'd had several secret meetings with Will and Turtle, treating them more as councilors than pages. The nursery closet was the most secure place they'd found.

What Turtle had said about the empress was true. She had held back when she should have gone forward. Earl Aubrey would have taken the chance. But the decision rested with Empress Matilda. Oxford was hers to command.

"What would happen if the empress surrendered?" asked Will.

"She cannot and will not do that," said Lady Elaine.

"What if she escaped?" asked Turtle.

"The king would pursue her," said Lady Elaine. "And that would mean relief for Oxford. For he cannot besiege and chase at the same time."

"Then we must contrive for her to leave," said Will.

"And if she doesn't go willingly, we can always toss her from the tower," said Turtle.

Lady Elaine laughed. She was enchanting; even the horrors of the siege couldn't destroy her loveliness.

"Landing on the frozen river, Her Imperial Highness would slide halfway to Wallingford," said Will.

Turtle laughed. But Lady Elaine grew serious. Had his jest offended her?

"I'm sorry, milady, if I've misspoken."

"Master Will," she said, her eyes brilliant in the torchlight. " 'Tis the beginning of a plan."

"I can see it!" said Turtle.

See what? thought Will, but he held his tongue.

"The empress could escape on the frozen river," said Turtle.

"And she could be lowered from the south side of the tower," said Lady Elaine. "Directly onto the river."

It *was* a plan, a wonderful plan!

"She could strap shinbones to her shoes and skate on the ice as we did with Edith," said Will.

"And the river would take her much of the way to Wallingford," said Lady Elaine. "Sir Brian can take her to Robert of Gloucester. And I doubt that the king will pursue her or attempt another siege this winter."

The king's supplies must be running low, too, though they had no shortage of firewood, keeping several bonfires going night and day. Will folded his arms, trying to warm his hands in his armpits.

"Would she consider such a plan?" asked Turtle.

"Her Imperial Highness does not lack for courage," said Lady Elaine.

Whatever else she may lack, thought Will.

"And she has *mentioned* the insufficiencies of Oxford Castle," said Turtle.

The empress, despite having the only comforts in the castle, complained constantly. The food was inedible, her chamber cold, the stench of sickness unendurable. It was unendurable, but not in her warm chamber, far from the misery of those who were dying in her defense.

"Yet it is much too dangerous. How could such an escape go unnoticed?" said Lady Elaine. "Even on the darkest night she could be plainly seen."

"It would take but a moment for her to be safely away," said Will.

"A moment is long enough for an arrow to find its mark," said Turtle.

They remained silent. It was a good plan and would be successful if only the empress could be made invisible. Will looked at Lady Elaine's face, pale as the winter moon, surrounded by her snow-white wimple. She would disappear in the snow-covered land. And so would the empress if she were wrapped from head to foot in white!

"What if the empress had a surcoat of bed linens?" asked Will. "What if she were all in white?"

"Her face veiled and even her hands gloved in white!" said Turtle, catching Will's excitement.

"Yes, dressed in white she could slip away unnoticed," said Lady Elaine. She looked hard at Will and Turtle. "Of course her guard and guides would need also be in white."

Will knelt at her feet.

"I will go, milady," he said.

"And I," said Turtle, kneeling beside him.

"It is a plan fraught with danger. But suited to you both, Master Will, Torrence," said Lady Elaine. "I believe you know the way to Wallingford as well as any. You are the only ones who could skate Her Imperial Highness down the river."

Will felt warm for the first time in weeks. This was his chance.

"Milady," said Will. "Edith has shown me a secret passage into the stables. The empress could slip into Wallingford unnoticed."

"And completely elude the king's grasp," said Lady Elaine. "I shall speak with the earl and Her Imperial Highness directly."

Would they agree to it? Would the empress trust two boys with the fate of England?

"Sir Rabbit," said Turtle. "You will be like the winter hare, changing your coat to beguile the hunters."

"As long as his heart remains steadfast and true," said Lady Elaine, "Master Will may don whatever color he chooses."

Somehow Lady Elaine convinced Earl Aubrey and

Empress Matilda of the plan. She said she had shamed the empress into it. Will found that hard to imagine.

It had also been agreed that a party of knights would simulate an escape from the postern gate, with one amongst them dressed as the empress, while the real empress was being lowered from the tower. The archers would create a further diversion, firing flaming arrows at the siege towers. The empress had wanted several armed knights to accompany her. But eventually, she agreed that clanking armor and weaponry might hinder her chance of escape.

Once the plan was agreed to, it was hurriedly put into effect. But all was done in utmost secrecy. All the ladies, even the Princess Von Holstein, were set to work, turning bed linens into hooded surcoats for the empress, Will, and Turtle. Sir Percival was tricked out to resemble the empress. Lady Marle sacrificed her tresses to make him a false plait. Will and Turtle salvaged some shinbones from the kitchen, boiled clean of their meat, and fashioned them into skates.

Early the next morning, they brought the skates to the empress.

"Well, which is the Rabbit and which is the Turtle?" she asked.

"Your Highness," said Lady Elaine, putting a hand on Will's shoulder. "This is Master William Belet, son of Sir John Belet of Blindley Heath, known to some as Rabbit."

Lady Elaine had never called him Rabbit.

"And this is Torrence of Cornwall, of the noble blood of Wales."

The empress smiled a mean smile, and Will felt Turtle stiffen.

"So he is the Turtle," said Empress Matilda.

"Their bynames belie the skills and courage of these young men. I trust Your Highness will not be misled by such trifles."

"I judge a man by his deeds," said the empress. "Let's get on with the lessons!"

At least she hadn't called them boys. They went to the top of the tower, which had been flooded with water and was now frozen solid. Turtle brought out the skates, and with the help of Lady Marle, they fastened them to the empress's fur-lined boots.

The crenelations along the tower had been boarded up to protect them from arrow shot and to keep the king's men in the siege tower from seeing what they were about. They were out of range of the catapults that launched the Greek fire and stones. So all they had to worry about was Her Imperial Highness's temper.

"You clumsy dolts!" she said, slipping on the ice. "You are not supporting me properly!"

She boxed Will's ears and dug her nails into his

shoulder. He remembered what fun it had been with Edith when he was learning how to skate — how hard they'd laughed. If Will laughed now, he was quite sure the empress would have his tongue cut out.

But Her Imperial Highness didn't give up. In fact, she surprised Will by how hard she worked at it. She slipped and slid, cursing Will and Turtle. And by the end of the day she was skating well enough to make it to Wallingford.

The next day they practiced in the morning and rested in the afternoon. Will and Turtle were given a full meal at sundown in the nursery closet. They had soup flavored with meat, bread with hard cheese, and good ale to drink. Many were going without their rations to give them this meal.

"Eat, Rabbit," said Turtle. "You'll never make it to Wallingford on an empty belly."

For the first time in weeks Will ate his fill, and then they slept until Lady Elaine woke them. Getting up in the middle of the night reminded Will of the matins service at Godstone. Perhaps even now Simon was rising from his bed to sing the midnight office. Will secured the cross Simon had given him in his girdle. Maybe Simon would think of him and say a prayer.

The castle was dark and still. Silently, Lady Elaine and Dame Catherine helped them on with their white robes and the linen strips that were wrapped around their dark wool leggings. They each had a small pouch filled with food and a dagger. Lady Elaine gave Will a letter for Lady Margaret. Before she brought them to the empress's chamber, Lady Elaine spoke to Will and Turtle with great solemnity.

"Neither the earl nor the empress will give you proper thanks for this deed. But I, Elaine, Countess of Oxford, daughter of the great house of Somerset, I thank you on behalf of all within these walls who will live because of the valor of Master William Belet and Squire Torrence of Cornwall."

Will was in an agony of embarrassment. And Turtle for once was completely discomposed.

Then she kissed each of them and brought them to the empress. Will followed her wimple, mothlike in the darkness. His head was reeling and his cheeks burned. His liege lady had done him a great honor. Please, God, he would be worthy of it.

The empress was dressed and ready. Lady Marle knelt at her feet and kissed her hand. The earl was with Sir Percival and the other knights at the postern gate. Will and Turtle put on their skates and assisted the empress, making sure that all were fastened securely. No one spoke. With a nod from the empress the servants doused the torches and removed the shutter from the south window. Lady Elaine embraced Will and Turtle and whispered, "God's speed!"

It had been decided that either Will or Turtle would precede the empress in case their deception failed. Will had drawn the first lot. He walked awkwardly on the shinbones to the window ledge where two stout knights tied his waist with rope from an enormous coil on the floor, and hefted him onto the casement. Will slipped easily through the narrow window and crouched on the sill.

The snow fields were still and silvered in the moonlight. The frozen Thames glimmered. A horse whinnied softly. There was no sign of the king's men. But Will's heart was thumping so hard in his chest, it might well be heard by any on duty below. He hadn't thought about the height before. It was a long way down to the river and there was no honor to be had in falling to his death from the tower. Finally he steadied himself enough to turn and nod to the knights. Lady Elaine had him fixed in her gaze, her hands clasped before her so tightly the knuckles were white. Will swung out and eased himself off the ledge into the frigid night. He clung to the rope, his own knuckles as white as the sheets. He murmured a prayer to St. Jude, as the knights let him down the awful distance to the river of ice.

XXIII.
The Winter Hare

Will landed with a jolt. His legs slid out from under him and he lay sprawled on the ice. His fingers fought with the knotted rope. He managed to free himself and get back on his feet — his skates. He signaled to the tower and they pulled up the rope. He'd made it down safely. But he wasn't safe. Standing in the middle of the frozen river, he was more exposed than ever. He tried to remember Lady Elaine's words of praise to drive away the fear that chilled him more deeply than the numbing black night.

Now they were lowering the empress. "Please God, let her hold her tongue," Will prayed. Dangling from the rope, surrounded by the dark, by unseen enemies . . . he knew how awful it was, and Her Imperial Highness wasn't inclined to suffer in silence. But just this once, she must keep quiet. Will was freezing, but dared not move an inch to warm himself. The king's guard might be watching the river, waiting for the slightest movement to loose their arrows. The night was colder than anything he could remember, even during the encampment at Lincoln. The fear, the waiting, was endless.

The empress was halfway down the tower. Her cloak blended in with the white stones, silver and milky in the moonlight. Even knowing where she was, Will had difficulty seeing her. Will hoped he was as inconspicuous, standing in the middle of the Thames. As Turtle had said, he was the winter hare, out in the open, depending on his coat for safety. But white fur and white robes were no protection from arrow or lance. The rabbit's fear threatened to engulf him.

"Help me, you dolt!" said the empress, in a harsh whisper. "Don't just stand there!"

He'd been so lost in his own fear, he'd not noticed her reaching the ice only a few feet from where he stood. He rushed to the empress, helped her get her balance, and untied the rope. He jerked the rope twice, signaling the knights to retrieve it. Turtle was let down much more quickly, never mind that he was bumped into the tower several times.

Just as Turtle was set down they heard the creak of the postern gate and the muffled sound of horses. The decoy knights were riding forth.

"Help me!" whispered Turtle. "Hurry!"

They untied the rope, sent it back up the tower, and began skating as fast as they could downriver toward

Wallingford. Within minutes, the alarm was sounded by the king's men. They'd seen the Oxford knights, and half the camp would be riding hell-for-leather after them.

"Now is the time for speed," said Turtle. "May we assist Your Imperial Highness?"

She nodded. Will and Turtle linked arms with her and skated faster than ever, pulling the empress along.

The harsh cold and icy fear tore through him, but at least now he was moving. He would outrun the king's men. He'd outrun his own fears. Now was the time to gain their advantage, the skaters and the knights. Their plan would work as long as the knights kept the king's men distracted and didn't get caught. But if the knights were caught, might not King Stephen suspect the true escape and pursue the empress that much more intently?

The king must know that the situation in Oxford Castle was desperate, and that Her Imperial Highness would bolt if she could. If they failed . . . if the knights failed . . . Empress Matilda would be in irons and all the hope of England crushed. For the knights, for Turtle and Will, death would be long and slow. They all must get as far away from Oxford as quickly as possible. Then Will need only worry about wolves and outlaws. The next moment, Will snagged a tree root. He completely lost his balance and crashed down on the ice, nearly bringing the empress with him.

"Stupid, clumsy boy!" she hissed.

Turtle gave him a hand and pulled him to his feet. Will winced as he put weight on his left foot.

"Can you still skate?" asked Turtle.

"I have to, don't I?"

Turtle shrugged.

"Come on, then," said the empress. "We must go!"

They started up again. This time the empress seemed to be supporting Will. His ankle throbbed, but each stroke forward was a step toward freedom. He wouldn't think about the pain. He'd keep his thoughts on Wallingford twelve miles away. Wallingford . . . safety.

They were about to cross under the bridge of the rheumy-eyed toll keeper. The old man had sheltered at Oxford Castle for the siege. No doubt the king's men were now collecting the toll. Would they notice three shadows passing under the bridge? Will's left foot caught on a ripple in the ice and he groaned. They'd certainly notice a noisy shadow. What wouldn't he give to be galloping to Wallingford on his little mare. Not that she could gallop now. She was skin and bones, and dull from hunger and lack of exercise. Once the siege was over, he'd make sure she had all the hay and oats she could eat. He'd see her grow fat and frisky. He'd —

"Rabbit!"

Will looked at Turtle. He'd been drifting into a dream and was likely to fall and twist his other ankle. The cold and his fear were numbing his ankle and everything else, including his brain.

The empress's cape and hood were lined with rich fur, as were her boots and gloves, but she would be cold, too. She didn't complain. She skated on and on. The darkness and her hood hid her face, but her whole being revealed an iron determination. She was very little, like the selfish, shrewish woman he'd seen at Oxford. But this woman skating next to him looked like the true heir of King Henry. Lady Elaine was right — she wasn't afraid to fight her battles. But could she win them? And if once she won the crown, would she have the strength and wisdom to keep it?

Turtle caught his eye. Will looked up. They were passing the charred remains of a wattle and daub hut on the riverbank. It had been the Herb Widow's home. She'd not made it to the safety of the castle walls. Will murmured a quick prayer. He hoped she'd died quickly.

They were nearly halfway to Wallingford. At the next bend in the river, Turtle signaled Will. It was time to set out across the snow-covered fields. They helped the empress to the riverbank and unstrapped her skates and theirs, burying them in the snowy bank.

They were all breathing heavily, and the hardest part of their journey was only just beginning.

"Your Imperial Highness," said Turtle, "this may be the best shelter we'll have until we reach Wallingford."

Ahead were open fields, with only a few thin copses for wind break.

"Then we shall rest here a moment," said the empress.

Will and Turtle poured wine for the empress and cut cheese, which they laid on a linen napkin.

"You eat, too," she said. "There is no time for ceremony."

They ate the hard yellow cheese and drank the warming wine. Will was just recovering his breath when the empress stood up, shaking out her skirts. Will rose to his feet and fell down immediately, struck by the searing white pain in his ankle.

Turtle bent over him, gently touching the swollen flesh.

"Well, you are the healer," he said. "What should we do?"

"Bind it tightly," said Will.

Turtle looked around at the snow and ice, as if there were bandages to be had on the riverbank.

"Cut off part of this bedsheet," said Empress Matilda, holding out the hem of her cloak. "It will only trip me up in the snow."

Turtle looked to Will. It was death to bring a blade so close to Her Imperial Highness's person. It was —

"Must I do it myself?" she asked.

"No, Your Imperial Highness," said Turtle. Shakily, he took out his dagger and sliced strips of cloth from the hem of her robe.

"You are most gracious, Highness," said Will.

"Get on with it," she said. "We must be moving."

She could have left him behind, even if he was the one who knew the secret entry to Wallingford. Traveling with a limping boy might be more of a hazard than banging on the gates at Wallingford.

Will helped Turtle wrap the bandage and they were soon heading across the moonlit fields. Far away a wolf howled. Will stumbled. The drifted snow masked all the ditches and hollows. They all tripped and floundered. Will's leggings were soaked through and crusted with ice. His legs, his face, his hands burned with cold. Each step seemed impossible. Her Highness was struggling with her skirts. She should have dressed as a man. It was taking them much too long to cross the fields. Should the morning sun catch them out in the open, they would stand out as plain as day, never mind that they were three winter hares.

What was it Lady Elaine meant when she said he might wear whichever color he chose? Was she telling him there was no disgrace in changing his allegiance from one lord to another? Lady Elaine might keep

Earl Aubrey from murdering him, but she couldn't insist that the earl promote Will or honor him with knighthood. In Oxford Will would always be Rabbit. Earl Aubrey could keep him a squire forever. And that might be worse than death. Perhaps Lady Elaine would return to Somerset. Will could follow her there, to the bishop's manse. But the bishop would want to make a clerk of him, not a knight. He could not be a scribbler his whole life long. He'd as lief be a squire.

Will stumbled into a ditch and found himself up to his chin in snow. His ankle was an agony. He was so very tired. He would just rest here and they could go on ahead.

"Get up!" said Turtle.

"Go on," said Will. "Let me stay here."

"Master William Belet," said Turtle, "you cannot abandon your duty and your liege lady!"

He sounded almost like Sir John or Peter of Redvers. And he'd called him Master William Belet! For a moment Will's head swam, trying to remember it all. Then he shook himself violently.

He must carry on. He was the one who knew the secret passage into Wallingford. He would not forsake his duty to the empress. He would prove himself worthy of his father's good name. Will fought his way out of the snow. Turtle took his hand and grimly smiled.

"Hurry!" said the empress.

The night sky was already paling.

They found a ridge, thinly coated with snow, and were able to walk sure-footedly. But now the empress was having trouble. The long trek had caught up with her. Will could make out her sharp features, straining with the effort of each step. Her breath came hoarse and raspy as she struggled on. Yet she fought her tiredness without complaint. Will helped support her as best he could, though Turtle bore the brunt of it. Perhaps they should cut away more of her sodden garments and reduce the weight she had to carry.

Black against the graying east rose the manor of Wallingford. It was at most a mile away. They could follow the ridge until they were abreast of the gate, and then they must plunge back into the snow fields. In the bramble hedge that surrounded the palisade was a slight opening that led to a hidden door into the bailey. It would look quite different now from when Edith had first shown it to him. What if he couldn't find the breach in the hedge? Three people dressed in white poking around the defenses would arouse suspicion. They might even be shot at by Sir Brian's guard.

Yet it was all worth the risk to keep their plan as secret as possible. Once rested, the empress could ride to Robert of Gloucester in a new disguise, and so slip safely beyond the king's grasp. If word got out that she was at Wallingford, it would bring upon them the full force of the king's levy. Wallingford could not withstand that for even one day.

One laborious footstep followed another, and another, and another. At last they were opposite the gate of Wallingford, where the ridge veered away from the manor. The sky was the color of lavender silk; little time was left before the sun rose on a cloudless day. Will nodded to Turtle.

"Your Highness," said Turtle. He, too, was breathing heavily, and his face was rimed with frost. "We must now cross the snow fields."

"Very well," she said, her voice dry and spent.

It was only some fifty yards to the hedgerow, though it seemed an eternity. There was no hurrying the empress. She was doing well just managing to keep upright. Will, himself, was barely moving. The snow was like a malevolent creature, dragging them down, keeping them from their safe harbor.

Fight it, thought Will. Fight it like a dragon or an evil knight. Don't let the snow win. Fight through it.

And somehow they did.

They reached the shadow of the hedgerow just as the golden sun stretched over the snow-bound land. Will found the concealed breach. There was one last struggle through the snow-drifted brambles. Then they slipped through the hidden door that led directly into the stables. Before Will could look for a blanket for Empress Matilda to lie on, she had collapsed on the warm, sweet hay. Will and Turtle fell nearby. And they lay there in the empty stall, listening to the soft whicker of horses, breathing in the gentle air.

XXIV.
Sir Rabbit

"You have rendered us a service, Master Rabbit. And we are not ungrateful." The empress spoke in a raspy whisper. Perhaps she was being cautious. Maybe it was all she could manage.

Will lay silent in the straw where Turtle had left them to go fetch Sir Brian. What could he say to her? Will pulled the rough blanket Turtle had found for them up around his shoulders. His teeth chattered, as the warmth from the straw and blanket wakened his frozen limbs. He'd rather have gone to find Sir Brian than remain with the empress, but Turtle didn't think a limping rabbit would slip unnoticed through the Fitz Count manor.

"So, Rabbit, what will be your reward?"

"I beg your pardon, Highness?"

"The reward for your service."

He looked at her for signs of mockery, but she seemed artless.

"It was only the service due to my liege lady," said Will.

"Perhaps I shall be queen, after all." She laughed dryly and then coughed. "At least I've led Stephen on a merry chase! So, boy, what *is* your wish?"

Will struggled to his knees. This was his chance, perhaps the only chance he'd ever have. He must not waste it.

"I mean no disrespect to my noble uncle, the earl of Oxford," said Will, trying to choose his words carefully. "But if I could, I would serve your son, Lord Henry Plantagenet."

The empress eyed him coldly.

"Best for a Belet to leave the house of de Vere," she said. "I will send you to Anjou when the weather softens and the winds favor a Channel crossing. Until then, will you remain at Oxford?"

He hadn't an answer to that. Fortunately Turtle arrived with Sir Brian and Lady Margaret, still in her night clothes. Sir Brian smiled broadly at Will, then fell to his knees beside the empress.

"Your Imperial Highness does my house the greatest honor."

Lady Margaret came forward, curtsied deeply, and kissed the empress's hand.

"Your Highness is half frozen," she said. "We will take you to finer quarters and get you some warm soup."

"You must keep me hidden," said the empress.

"Torrence of Cornwall has explained everything," said Sir Brian. "We'll take you directly to our chamber where you may rest behind drawn curtains."

The empress nodded.

"You will have to get two stout men to carry me," she said. "I cannot walk another step."

"Permit me," said Sir Brian. He moved forward and swept her into his arms.

Will wondered how they would manage to cross the bailey unnoticed as he tried to get to his own feet. He fell back immediately into the straw. Lady Margaret came to his aid.

"Rest, Master Will," she said. "We'll return for you soon. Meanwhile I'll send Edith to you with food and a draught."

Will settled back against the straw, his ankle throbbing, and let Lady Margaret cover him with the horse blanket.

"We are so very proud of you, Master Will," she said, then hurried out after Sir Brian.

Turtle knelt beside Will and offered him a flagon of wine.

Will drank deeply, letting the warmth slide down his throat. He grinned at Turtle.

"We made it," said Will. "Did you work a spell for us, Turtle of Cornwall?"

Turtle laughed.

"Yes," he said. "I made the snow white, the night dark and colder than the devil's heart. Was it not clever of me?"

Will laughed, too, then stopped.

"Do you think the decoy knights outran the king's men?"

"It seems more likely that they rode to their deaths," said Turtle.

"God grant they died with their swords drawn," said Will.

"I believe they considered themselves lucky," said Turtle. "They died for England."

So many had died and so many more might die before the crown of England was secured.

"Shall Oxford Castle be released?" asked Will.

"The earl and king will parley. In the end Earl Aubrey will probably agree to an immense tribute paid by the suffering of peasants. The king may also demand hostages."

Would Lady Elaine have to give up her little son to appease the king? Or would he be satisfied with the tribute? Will could not leave Oxford if his lady was sore troubled.

"Master Will," said Turtle. "We have succeeded in our plan. You may rest on that for now. Do not hurry to greet the future's ills, which will arrive soon enough anyway."

Will smiled.

"What would you choose if the empress offered you a reward?" he asked.

Now Turtle smiled.

"She offered a boon, did she? Well then, I shall have a snow-white mare and a Welsh manor."

Turtle looked at Will.

"And you. You chose the Plantagenet."

Will nodded.

"What did I tell you? Miracles can happen — even in England."

Turtle took a drink of the wine.

"Master Will, you have done well for yourself and your family," he said. "The empress is loyal to her supporters. She will be the patron and protector of you and your family from now on. Earl Aubrey will not dare harm any of the Belets, nor make further claims on Blindley Heath."

Turtle leaned forward, grinning.

"You will be Sir Rabbit after all."

"Sir Rabbit," said Edith, arriving with a laden tray. "It suits, and the white hare can be the device on your shield."

It was the first he'd seen of Edith since the autumn, and even in the dim light of the stable he could see she'd grown pale and somber, despite her teasing words.

"Turtle," she said. "Get you to my mother's chamber, where you'll find warm food and a waiting bed.

Father will come soon for Will. I shall pour some warmth into him while he waits. Later, once you're both rested, you can bring Uther and Maiden to visit Will."

"How are they?" asked Will.

"Uther howled for four straight days, he was so lonesome for you. You're lucky my father spared him," said Edith.

"Naturally, my Maiden was too refined to make a fuss," said Turtle.

"Naturally," said Edith.

Before he left, Turtle awkwardly patted Will's shoulder.

"Take leave of your worries, Master Will," he said. "Rest now and grow strong."

Edith helped Will sit up and spoon fed him the warm broth.

"I can manage on my own," he said.

"For now, *you* are the patient. Try to *be* patient."

"Very well," said Will. He settled back, avoiding Edith's sad eyes. The soup was good, and he'd finally stopped shivering. His fingers and toes prickled and stung. It was a welcome sign that there was no frostbite. After the soup he'd get Edith to help him with his ankle. They'd need to loose the binding and —

"Master Will," said Edith. "Remember when first we met?"

"Aye," said Will.

"How I longed for my future?"

Will nodded.

"It is settled," she said, and sighed. "I am to marry Sir Bohemund."

"Of Surrey?" asked Will.

Edith nodded.

"But he is so old!" said Will.

"Old," said Edith, "but noble and kind. My father has made me an honorable match."

"You can't —" began Will.

"Don't," said Edith. "I have nothing to complain of. I am the youngest daughter, and my portion is small."

Will was silent. He took another sip of broth and choked. So that was the change in Edith. He'd known all along that one day Edith would have to marry. He could not even hope to be her betrothed; what could he offer her? And yet he had hoped that some day he would have something to offer, that *he* might be her future.

She looked at Will with tears staining her dark eyes.

"I will soon be gone to Woburn Abbey. My new lord asked that I spend our betrothal amongst the holy sisters, learning to read and reckon," she said. "I think he wants to make sure I am quite tame before we wed next Michaelmas."

"Tamed!" said Will. "No one can tame a Fitz Count. Think of Simon."

Edith smiled.

"Thank you, Will, I'll do that."

Edith put down the spoon and took Will's hand. This would be their moment of leave-taking, their story ended before it had begun.

"You will have a fine manor," said Will.

"Aye, and if I am lucky, fine sons. And you, Will?"

"My future is settled as well," he said. "I will go to France to serve Henry Plantagenet."

"Father says he is a likely lad, a worthy heir to King Henry."

"He is a lord worth following. I think he will bring peace to England."

"When you are in Anjou, tilting at French dragons, will you remember us, Sir Rabbit?"

Will looked at her teasing eyes, so like Simon's. France was far away, but he'd not be there forever. Henry Plantagenet would return to fight for England with Will at his side. Will would always belong to England. How could he forget all the life he'd lived, the good, green land, the ones he loved?

"I'll remember," said Will. "I shall always remember."

THE END

Epilogue

Empress Matilda made it safely to the West Country where she stayed for five years, her power slowly ebbing. Soon after Robert of Gloucester died in 1147, she retired to Normandy.

The fight for the crown of England was carried on by Lord Henry, starting in 1147, when he was only fourteen. When he was sixteen, his father, Geoffrey of Anjou, named him duke of the conquered Normandy. In 1153 Duke Henry invaded England with a large force. That same year Eustace, son and heir of King Stephen, died suddenly. The lords and great churchmen of England negotiated a truce, leaving Stephen the throne as long as he lived, but granting the succession to Duke Henry. Within a year King Stephen was dead.

Henry II was king! Through his marriage to the Duchess Eleanor of Aquitaine Henry gained the largest Duchy in the south of France. He was not only king of England but duke of Aquitaine and Normandy, and Count of Anjou. Henry II fulfilled the hopes and expectations of all who had fought on his behalf. His long rule brought peace, order, and prosperity to England.

Author's Note

The plot of *The Winter Hare* closely follows the history of the time as outlined in the Laud Manuscript of the Anglo-Saxon Chronicle, which was written during the twelfth century at the monastery of Peterborough. The *Anglo-Saxon Chronicle* is an extraordinary document available to twentieth-century readers of English history. Oddly enough the chronicle was written in the vernacular at a time when *all* important documents, especially those emanating from the cloister, were written in Latin. I have used the *Anglo-Saxon Chronicle* as translated and edited by G. N. Garmonsway (Everyman) as well as numerous other sources to order the events of *The Winter Hare* and make my story as true to the historical record and the flavor of the medieval period as possible.

Briefly, these are the events described in the annals:

In 1137, when Stephen of Blois usurped the crown from his cousin, Empress Matilda, daughter of King

Henry and rightful heir, England was plunged into a devastating civil war that lasted nineteen years. Many unscrupulous barons took advantage of this troubled time, plundering the countryside. Villages, abbeys, churches, and ill-defended manors fell victim to their rapaciousness. Such evil walked the land that it was said "Christ and his Saints slept."

Once an ally, Earl Ranulf of Chester fell out with King Stephen. The king besieged the earl at his castle in Lincoln. Word was sent to Robert of Gloucester, half brother of Empress Matilda, who came with great levies to Chester's aid. On February 2, 1141, Candlemas day, Robert's men captured King Stephen and put him in irons.

Later that year, Empress Matilda and Robert of Gloucester were besieged at Winchester by an army led by King Stephen's queen, also named Matilda (to avoid confusion in my story I've called her Maude, a common diminutive of Matilda). While escaping from the starving city, Robert of Gloucester, in an effort to protect Matilda, was captured by Queen Maude's forces.

Empress Matilda was then taken to Oxford by her loyal barons and given the city to be her stronghold. Meanwhile an exchange of prisoners was negotiated, and both King Stephen and Robert of Gloucester were set free. The king besieged Matilda in Oxford. She escaped at night, let down by ropes from Oxford tower, and made her way on foot to Wallingford.

Accounts other than the *Anglo-Saxon Chronicle* say that the empress and the few men who accompanied her were cloaked in white to blend in with the snow-covered landscape. Although records show twelfth-century boys skated on the Thames in London, it is my invention that Empress Matilda skated to freedom on the frozen river.

There was a real John Belet, who was butler to Henry I and held a manor in Surrey. There also existed an Aubrey de Vere, who as Master Chamberlain was one of the most important ministers of Henry I. *His* son acquired an earldom, and de Veres were earls of Oxford until 1604. Sir Brian Fitz Count held Wallingford manor and was a staunch supporter of Matilda. I doubt that any of these men were the least bit like the characters in *The Winter Hare*.

My story is built upon that which is true. However, Will, Turtle, Edith, Simon, the evil earl, the fair Elaine, d'Artois, and Squat Wat are all fictions spun out of my fascination with a time so long ago and yet so vivid one can almost taste it.